When the Saints Come Marching In

Short fiction which takes a long view of the human
parade in its foolishness and fidelity.

by

James G. Powers

Kimera Publishing
Spokane, WA, USA

Acknowledgments

Ms. Linda Marie McDonald. Secretary extraordinaire, whose reliability, eye for details, and clear organization make her singularly invaluable.

Dr. Tod Marshall. For his generous gifts of time, infectious enthusiasm, and unerring judgment. These have shaped one whose calling is not unlike Swift's: "To mend the world."

Cover Photo: The photo in question is placed at: http://aboriginalcollections.ic.gc.ca/veterans/gallery/000 18.htm. The photo is part of the Native Veterans Association of Northwestern Ontario Web Site. It comes from over 15 years of photographs collected by David-Michael Thompson in researching the subject for those veterans rarely mentioned outside of their own family circles. We would also like to mention the soldier and the town he is from : Denis DeLaronde; Left row - third man, wearing a cowboy hat; From Red Rock, Ontario, Canada.

For further information, contact
kimera@js.spokane.wa.us
To order a copy of this book , send $10. to
N. 1316 Hollis, Spokane WA 99201

Table of Contents

Introduction: *The Saints Come Marching In!*

𝔄 reader who makes an acquaintance with these short stories will, necessarily, encounter a cluster of characters with unique values and views. These may exert either a shaping influence for good or a hostile influence for evil on one's life. The fiction writer, with some deftness, peering into the human soul, may trace this evolution through befuddling mazes and dizzying defiles. P.D. James, master of the mystery genre, provides a superlative example of this strategy.

Beyond characterization, short fiction can boast of considerable episodic detail. Not simply is it an iteration of historical record and truncated specifics; rather, this genre commands use of a gift which has been praised since Aristotle, namely, *mimesis*. This is committed to giving stark history a maximum enhancement, universal coloration, and a bigger than life attraction. Who can forget Dido's murals which moved Aeneas and his fellow exiles to see in and see beyond the world of Carthage? We find there a representational sign capable of cutting through "time zones" and also letting us step over "boundaries" which can severely limit our expansion of awareness.

In addition to successful characterization and episode, these narratives can also be said to celebrate language. Each of my short stories puts emphasis on words, not only as they tease a reader to keep turning the pages, but to see in a lively vocabulary a drawing of an ample picture, coaxing

us to view the human parade with wit and gentle satire. The Eighteenth Century, with giants like Henry Fielding, notably strove to refine language, believing it to be the mark of an authentic gentleman whose legitimate place was in the Age of Reason. Subsequent to this rhetorical deposit, language has, in many instances, fallen upon hard times, having drifted to serve as a toy for the banal, a chaperon for the illiterate, and an interpreter for modern quandary who confounds us by a kind of hurried, facile explication, capable of holding at bay clear thought and expression.

Much is bruited about concerning contemporary materialism whose devotees invest only the measurable with truth. If the "matter at hand" cannot be validated by something akin to "Safeway's scales," materialists insist such fraudulent reality should be tossed into the rubbish with all the dispatch with which one would fling a kitty's litter box! They conclude this is a fitting end for anything purporting to be associated with the intangible, the spiritual, the transcendent: goblins all without a basis.

But these stories take the opposite view against those who caterwaul exclusively for materiality. Skeptics are contested at every turn; they must compete with the saints themselves whose intrusions into human affairs are unmistakable, as vital as was their pilgrimage on earth. Briefly, it must be noted that an ordered world, ultimately, permits no rewards where not earned. As part of the harmonious scheme of things, the saints, by

presence if nothing else, discourage, if not frustrate, the undeserving from getting their way. Their modus operandi can be perceived as stern, but always fair. A "Salutation of Saints!" therefore, provides a provocative sub-title to this family of fiction.

The Wings of Moab: The Friendly Skies

Eglon of Philadelphia

Eglon Morsel learned to ignore others' dismal view of him. He was resigned that his potential was limited to one acquisition: obesity. To this end, he gloriously reigned over beef, bread, and bottle, from whose company he was rarely absent.

Eglon came by his tempestuous taste buds honestly; his mother, a devotee of bed and board herself, would have felt remiss were her son not equally committed to stomping out hunger with all the zeal of a Vista volunteer. Daisy Morsel, whose family once boasted three rotund progeny, now reduced to Eglon, had long allowed that it was impossible to serve two appetites at once: a spiritual hunger and "the only one that mattered." Briefly, there was no contest when it came to "feasting" with the Bible or cutting loose in a bakery!

This is not to say that Daisy ignored the Testament entirely. She carefully culled, as from a spice rack, Biblical names to suit her young porkers. The two deceased dumplings were appropriately called Salome and Ham, since their appetites too were notoriously tuned. But her progeny Eglon's provocative name constituted a triumph for Daisy's imagination. The Book of Judges held the answer: Eglon, paunchy King of Moab, represented quintessential sensuality.

Especially was this evinced in courtiers staring dumfounded at the spongy troughs of fat lavishly hanging down his middle. Through these, like into a canal, streams of sweat meandered while he squatted in the coolest recesses of his palace. His demise was fashioned for prime time: Ehud, the left-handed prophet, plunged his sword deep within the flaccid folds of Eglon's belly, which, like everything it contacted, ingested the blade and hilt as effortlessly as a carrot stick.

It was not King Eglon's shabby finale that prompted Daisy to confer the hapless monarch's name on her "youngest cupcake"; rather the Moabite's zest for the good life, from port to pomegranates, dictated Daisy's nomination.

Sundry sanctuaries of hedonism where special homage might be paid to their perforated ancestor were devoutly and yearly patronized by the corpulent couple. One undisputed enclave always emerged as THE elite Eden. Snuggled in the Allegheny Mountains of Southeastern Pennsylvania, on the outskirts of a town enterprisingly named Hollidaysburg, lies Sussex's Sybaritic Spa, vulgarly classified by angular scrawny folk as a "fat farm." Unlike its competitors, this paradise strained all its resources to knead sprawling poundage, to pamper every orifice, to fondle every dimple.

Each August, Eglon leaned on the counter of Allegheny Airlines negotiating first class tickets ("Who can perch on economy seats no bigger than a frying pan?") for a flight to "Elysium." When the day arrived for their march into the "Promised Land," Eglon, with his mother in tow, wheezed and

careened down the articulated arm leading into the aircraft. The steel artery moaned and heaved like a conveyor belt loading Amtrak engines. The two happy pilgrims inched by a slightly over-whelmed stewardess, who furtively glimpsed at the craft's wings, while murmuring patches of an act of contrition which the nuns tried to drill into 8th grade girls' distracted heads!

Snugly ensconced in their plush surroundings, soon after a take-off which vindicated American technology, mother and son plunged into Allegheny's "party favors," as Daisy delicately saluted the parade of hors d'oeuvres which she and Eglon intercepted with all of the gentility and dispatch of attack dogs!

But all festivity proved premature! A volley of curses and threats dented the air! Three maniacal hijackers, peering behind ski masks like riled raccoons, burst upon the sedate first class contingent, leaving an equal number of confederates to subdue the stunned economy section.

Dividing between them "persuaders" of glycerin and guns, the confederates, in fractured English, shrieked for quiet, promising swift silence for any who thought obedience was optional. When the senior stewardess, propelled ahead of the leader, staggered into the cockpit, the captain quickly learned that Allegheny Air was playing host to more than ordinary holiday revelers.

A radical, outlawed wing of Jewish extremists, for whom life held the value of a trinket, commandeered the craft for purposes larger than depositing customers on oases such as the Morsels luxuriated in! All frivolity was lost in the

magnitude of lethal, albeit outrageous, demands:
(1) a healthy ransom for their American captives,
held hostage over the last parcel of Yankee soil
some may put their feet upon; (2) a public pledge
never to relinquish the Golan Heights and yield
other strategic territory to Palestinians and their
"vile patron," the Syrians; (3) the release from
Israeli jails of "patriots" whose only crime lay in
supporting "true Jewish principles."

World crises and larger issues invariably
coasted by Daisy Morsel's immediate grasp. She
recklessly blurted: "See here, my son and I are on
our way to Hollidaysburg for a vacation. We
intend to go there too without your interference!"
With a searing glower and moving not a dime's
thickness from her mottled nose, the leader
rasped: "Yes, Mama Cow!" And pointing to the
emergency door, "We'll oblige you both. Just tell
us when! Nothing could please us more than to
empty two tubs of lard on that garbage heap you
call home!" Tangled between amazement and
anger, Daisy prodded Eglon to "do anything!" But
"Elephant Hero," as one hijacker taunted him,
remained still as a January floe. Only his jowls
quavered, like a bloated carp battling for air.

Between Philadelphia International,
Washington D.C., and Tel Aviv, negotiations
sputtered along, flaring in spurts, with strident
threats and commands. The Israeli fanatics
unlocked a careful, albeit procrustean, plan,
culminating in a landing at Tel Aviv, where it was
hoped, on a world stage, their drama of prosper or
perish would debut. Concessions surfaced, not
without ambiguity. To Israel, finally, Allegheny

Air was ordered; coordinates were computed, landing clearances and protection pledged. Thus it was that the Morsels veered away from Hollidaysburg, first to Havana, then, across the Atlantic, to Dakar in Senegal; next, a northerly pattern to Cairo. At last, languishingly slow, the DC 10 began its descent to Israel.

Daisy and Eglon, though seasoned travelers, verged on exhaustion. Their trauma was not lessened by the desiccated sandwiches tossed at them. Besides, when Daisy learned that their destination was the Holy Land, she sank deeper into despair. "The last place on earth I want to see," she gasped. Her imagination conjured up decaying shrines, cavernous churches, and processions of fasting monks.

Abrupt refusal to land at Tel Aviv, indeed on any Israeli soil, infuriated the conspirators, who felt betrayed; however, this reversal did not abort their plans. A strategy emerged to land on an abandoned military strip, in Jordan, whose ancient capital, ironically, was called Philadelphia. Touchdown was near the Gulf of Aquaba, within sight of Israeli territory. This wrinkled, scarred area, Al' Aqabah, in Biblical times, bowed to the rule of King Eglon, and it was known as Moab!

Though Solomon's mines are located scant miles north of the landing strip, reaches of desolation stretched like ropy tendons in every direction, hardened by scorching rays which licked the plane's interior when its doors yawned and the hapless hostages disembarked. They were permitted to seek refuge under the craft's wings from the pitiless desert blaze.

A wizened wisp of a man, a Jew, it happened, huddled close to Eglon, availing himself of the additional shade. His lips seemed to be in timorous dialogue with each other: *May you receive a full reward from the Lord, the God of Israel. / Under whose wings you have come to take refuge!*

With swirls of sweat beading down every fleshy recess in his body, a befuddled Eglon gasped: "What . . . what did you say?"

"An ancestor of mine once lived in these parts. .. name was RUTH. They were all starving . . . . The Lord sent one of his servants Boaz . . . . That was his prayer . . . . The WINGS reminded me . . . ."

Daisy, nudged her son, "He's delirious. Never mind. Poor thing!" But Eglon, choked with sand, simply stared beyond her, had he known it, in the fertile direction of Aqaba's gulf waters.

Veteran Israeli commandoes surrounded the plane, realizing their mission was no Entebbe. Resolutely, the troopers rejected all demands. Tempers shortened. A standoff seethed. Caught, as in a sheep-fold, the hostages, first stared anxiously at their captors, who hovered menacingly over their pawns, then squinted at their would be rescuers, whose granite expressions suggested they were "saving" them only for death.

Then it was, with stunning agility, Eglon, on his feet, hurled his lumpish frame at two terrorists. Instantly, bullets danced across the doughy floor of his belly, which seemed to absorb them as harmlessly as it would gumdrops. He blundered relentlessly on, toppling cumbrously against two killers whose guns mindlessly

continued to spatter his stomach like one would tamp jam into a waffle. Each assailant sprawled grotesquely beneath the bulk across him. The tumble, the distraction, were all the loyal Israeli forces needed to riddle their enemy into deafening silence.

Through bewildered eyes, the survivors and troops followed Eglon, hushed, as he pulled himself awkwardly, grievously beneath the shadow of the airliner. There, gently cradling his wounds, he gazed up at the awesome span. His eyes brightened; the grimace softened. And not a soul missed his five final words: "THE WINGS . . . OH! THE WINGS!"

Saint Peter's Fish: Catch of the Day
A Sweet Treat

The Soul that rises with us,
Our life's Star,
Hath had elsewhere its setting.

Wordsworth
"Intimations of Immortality"

To credit the poet's faith in pre-existence, one need search no further than the lives of Verna and Valeria O'Fally. Doubtless, earlier, each had the swimmingly good fortune to be a fish! Born twin Pisces, March 23rd, on the feast of the martyred Bishop Polycarp, these two sterling spinsters had enjoyed eighty years of uninterrupted bliss. Their parish church was Saint Peter's, where, daily, each piously attended the seven o'clock Mass. When he was alive and brimming with creative juices, Monsignor Nathaniel Landing prepared many meaty homilies which always proved a special treat. But none stirred their appetite so much as the pastor's unrivaled "Soup Du Jour" reflection on the "Miraculous Catch of Fishes."

To be sure, these two siblings, at some cost, maintained an ocean home, near Seaside, Oregon. At one time, ten years earlier, they experimented with boarders, but soon found the responsibility too burdensome.

"Perhaps we were too fussy," mused Verna.

"Older guests need more care than we could provide," added Valeria, "and then, the two

gentlemen dying, exactly right here, within a year
. . . ."

Both agreed they had learned a lesson; more
frugality, but fewer responsibilities, spelled a
happy "recipe."

Verna and Valeria rarely quarreled, unless, of
course, over a preference between Dover and
Petrale sole for Seafood Florentine. Verna
conceded that Petrale was considerably firmer but
was "tasteless as a pot holder." Valeria remained
skeptical; she would not give a nickel for an entire
English Channel catch (and here she showed her
Irish bias) even if "they threw the Queen in with
the bargain."

The two rarely left the haven of their residence
for any protracted time, especially since that
memorable tour to Rome and the Holy Land,
conducted by the "late Monsignor" some three
years ago. It was at Tiberias, on Lake Galilee, as
they often recounted the tragedy, that "Our Dear
Shepherd 'put out to sea.'" The doleful reference
looked to the priest's fatal tumble from a rock
promontory, where he was last seen.

Investigators hazarded that the good man, who
had shown some signs of fatigue in recent months,
must have been meditating alone one evening,
when he lost his footing on the ropy moss and
slipped into the turbulence below. Authorities
never fished him out. Though the ugly incident
marred the rest of the journey, forcing the ladies to
hasten home, the fact that their pastor departed in
such an irenic setting, on a pilgrimage no less,
muted their sorrow. "He was undoubtedly gazing
across at that picturesque church on the Mount of

Beatitudes when he was taken from us," murmured Valeria.

"Yes. Just think of it! 'Blessed are the poor in spirit . . . '," added her twin, dabbing her eyes.

Both spinsters still recalled their uneasy luncheon at the "Twelve Apostles' Bark," in Tiberias, the day of the calamity. The pilgrims were heartily encouraged to try the restaurant's specialty: Saint Peter's Fish!

"Very ugly but a sweet treat," enthused the proprietor. Neither sister had to be persuaded further; their predilection for seafood, not to mention loyalty felt for their parish patron saint, who, with his friends, fished in these waters, prompted a quick consent.

"I just hope it hasn't been on ice since the Apostles' Creed!" chuckled Monsignor Landing. "There's nothing worse than rancid fish," shivered the pastor.

When the vaunted dish arrived, a glowering, saw-jawed, fierce-eyed specimen, with clay-pocked skin to match its sullen appearance and seeming longevity, all diners gaped in mild trepidation. Soon, however, they braved its forbidding stare and cut into its succulent, delicately textured meat.

"This only shows you not to judge from the outside. Still, I must eat it with my eyes closed," teased Verna. Despite her titters, the fixed scowl of the creature pestered her imagination. Months later, she would describe it as if it were wriggling on the plate, inviting the curious to its noiseless world of briny secrets.

The young curate, Father E. Patrick Curraugh, assigned two years before to assist Monsignor Landing's successor at Saint Peter's, never for a moment considered himself anything but feverishly relevant. He habitually salted his rather bland diet of theology with two favorite adverbs: "really" and "very" as if these little helpers would add in sincerity what was lacking in substance. The O'Fally's still cluck disapprovingly of his introductory homily at Sunday Mass:

"Hi! I'm Father Curraugh, but I really want you to call me 'E. Pat'. I'm really very, very happy to share my call with you and really want you to share yours with me. Really!"

"Gracious!" whispered Verna. "He wants to know who is phoning us?"

E. Pat lurched ahead. "I've discerned with Tracy Spills, our bishop, you know, to come here and share parish poverty, parish misery, parish loneliness and sickness and pain as a co-pastor with Len Stalk, our 'Chief Presider.'"

Father Linus Stalk, the pastor, finally raised an eyebrow, revealing that he was not wearing a death mask. News of a "co-pastor" role came as a bit of a surprise after several years of laboring under a different illusion. He was also curious to learn if parish boundaries included more than Saint Agnes' Hospital and Henning's Mortuary.

"The main deal," chattered E. Pat," is to love . . . and, of course, that's really to share, to love. I know many come here just to attend Mass and be reconciled -- you know, confession. However, none of these things can replace love . . . that's the real sacrament . . . when we share. Thanks! I very

day in my life. Now we can get back to sharing the bread . . . ."

"I wonder if that . . . interesting young man likes fish," confided Verna.

"I doubt it," murmured her sister. "He's probably a hot dog person. Still, let's invite him soon."

Father Linus Stalk always prided himself on his patience; however, in the last two years, bombarded by Father Curraugh's effusions, he found that virtue sorely tested.

"I'm disgusted with his 'jump ball' theology!" he would grumble to clerical cronies. "He wouldn't recognize an absolute if one jumped on his lap and asked to marry him!" The pastor fired another salvo across Father Curraugh's bow: "I swear to God if E. Pat thought it was trendy to grow a tail, he'd be first in line to soak his fanny in a bucket of Ortho and cut a hole in his britches to boot to welcome the accessory!"

It would appear that this recent tirade was traceable to his assistant's timely homily the preceding Sunday, where, for a ten o'clock Mass, a slightly bewildered flock had struggled into church to be treated to a "Consumer Society's Sense of God." Later, the curate explained, "This is where the people are at. We've got to go through their door to tackle the Lord, so that He really grabs them."

The success of this somewhat dubious wrestling match between the Father and His Faithful depended on an advertising litany which sought to exhort consumer Catholics to probe God's Nature in depth -- a goal previous thinkers over 2,000

years apparently had failed to accomplish. "What is God like?" queried E. Pat, squinting over his audience with the triumphal gaze of an explorer who had just discovered lost Atlantis:

God is like Coca-Cola:
"He's the real thing!"

God is like Pepsi:
"He's got a lot to give!"

God is like a Chevrolet:
"He's building a better way."

God is like a Dodge:
"You can depend on Him."

God is like Hallmark cards:
"He cares enough to send the very best."

God is like Dial soap:
"He gives you 'round the clock protection."

God is like Alka-Seltzer:
"Try him! You'll like Him!"

"Ah well," groused Father Stalk, skulking into the sacristy, "he'll soon be off the premises for a couple weeks, on vacation. Thank you, God!"

When E. Patrick Curraugh sprinted up the immaculate steps leading to the O'Fally's door, he anticipated his visit for two reasons: to study these charmingly eccentric ladies while feasting on their

renowned cuisine; and to absorb some tips for his
own forthcoming trip to the Holy Land.

On neither account was E. Pat to be
disappointed. Greeted politely at the door, the
ebullient assistant was hospitably ushered into the
living room for appetizers of Dungeness crab and
marinated Quilcene oysters, rinsed away by a
subtle chenin blanc from neighboring
Washington's Latah Vineyards. The main entrée
celebrated the Northwest's Chinook salmon,
bathed in Dijon mayonnaise, dill weed, and coaxed
to life in Chablis, with a poaching secret both
women vied to divulge.

Finishing this repast, Curraugh raptured: "It's
the very, very best dinner I'll probably ever eat.
Really!"

Valeria and Verna, always reserved, were
flattered by his fulsome praise, plying him with
second and third servings. "Eat and be contented,
Father . . . . I hope you don't mind the title . . . .
The good Lord provides us all with limited time
but wants it full of much joy."

Despite his euphoria, the priest perceived that
his hosts were amazingly alert, sturdy souls,
whose vivid recollection of their earlier tour was
extraordinarily helpful: tips to provide, taxis to
hail, hotels to negotiate, sites to visit all were
spelled out and duly noted. E. Pat sat in
admiration at his elderly parishioners' grasp of
details which contrasted with his truncated view of
the past. When he rose to depart, his stomach and
head were filled to their limited capacity.

"One final suggestion, Father . . . E. Pat,"
timidly stammered Valeria, "though it will be

painful, do visit the seaside promontory where Monsignor Landing took his leave. You shouldn't get lost. It would mean so much. And say a prayer on our behalf. We have felt his absence so."

Departing, Father Curraugh, in an artesian burst of appreciation, kissed both ladies on the cheek and found himself cuddling a small farewell gift. "It's our special candy, Father . . . rather medicinal. One, daily, should find you as healthy as a freshly caught trout. Good night and may the good Lord keep you always on his fishing line!"

For the young, impressionable tourist the week abroad surged along scarcely noticed. He followed the Scala Sancta in Jerusalem's walled city; strolled silently between Golgotha and Christ's tomb under the roof the Holy Sepulchre; marveled at the Dome of the Rock; knelt at the star embedded in Bethlehem's Nativity Shrine; and now, after a meal in Tiberias, Father E. Patrick Curraugh stood pensively, balanced on a promontory, looking across Galilee's troubled waters, in the direction of the Mount of Beatitudes.

Dusk, punctured by a declining sun, which skittered between bullying clouds, absorbed E. Pat's frenetic soul, plunging him into a reflective silence: "I guess one can share alone," he breathed. Somehow, he felt dramatically altered, not isolated, but joined together, of a piece, like those miraculous mosaics in Nazareth's basilica.

He turned to permit the stiff breeze to stroke his back. As he did so, his head tilted, and his eyes first strained, then arrested, and finally widened with the same unblinking gaze of Saint Peter's Fish. A hoarse, guttural cry clutched his throat:

"No! Can't be! Impossible! It's a mistake! He's ... "
Intending to step forward but instead, stumbling
backwards, Curraugh lost his balance, slid to one
knee, and pitched helplessly, hopelessly, into the
devouring surf.

A man, escorting a deliciously young girl,
glanced up, distracted by the muffled clamor. He
moved his eyes briefly from his raven treasure to
the vacant shore. Despite his sandy wig and
youthful slacks, despite his brisk step and
vivacious appearance, the gentleman had to be
Monsignor Nathaniel Landing.

Saint Drogo's Budding Banker
Pennies from Heaven

Father Amos Drogo Strutt, also given the breezy sobriquet of "Your Grace" by his clerical contemporaries, was snoring hoarsely in his backyard hammock. At a distance, the whole sleepy setting resembled a plump German sausage incongruously stretched between two tree limbs. It would be impossible to say what, over the years, had shaped Amos' ambiguous character and finally released it from this world's grasp! "Your Grace" Strutt had managed to veneer and disguise his homegrown, dour personality by a congenial mask, a kind of "born again" bonhomie capable of beguiling an innocent observer. Any witness would perceive little of the rooted rapacity which blighted the priest's character and rutted his pilgrim's path until, suddenly, his journey was cut short under circumstances as cloudy as the skies which provided a canopy for his funeral procession. Though named after Saint Drogo, Flemish patron of pilgrims, the saint's abiding protection for Amos' spotty itinerary was not easily deciphered.

Strutt came from a Wisconsin family of Belgian immigrants. They were four in number: the father, mother, sister and Amos. All were loners; each seemed obsessively private. Even when an emergency struck, they usually scribbled hurried notes to each other. Only then, to be understood, would each blurt some emaciated announcement or terse explanation; however, this compromise

was as infrequent as chatter in a Cistercian monastery. This is not to suggest that the family's peculiarities focused only on laconic grunts; other intriguing crotchets visited the Strutt household, and these whimsies piqued considerable interest in their neighbors, provoking skimpy sympathy and much ridicule. In fairness, it must be said that the family possessed an almost simian-like mimicry of polished, cultivated society which permitted it to behave, on demand, nearly civilized. The father, Osgood "Boss" Strutt, especially preened himself on his brand of social suavity. "I can put on the dog as good as those swells I can't avoid in Mass," he would crow. The parish he alluded to was dedicated to Saint Francis Assisi, who must have flinched in his beatific discourse, when referring to "Boss" as "Brother Osgood." In fact, reviewing the heavenly record of one's salvation, mournful, ministering angels would have to tag as zero Boss Strutt's chances of "paradisal promise"!

Elzora Strutt, stumpy matriarch of the family, had contended for years with Parkinsonian Syndrome. Elzora, comfortable only with solidities and fixed reality, admonished the doctor who discovered her problem six years earlier: "You can call it a 'syndrome' if you want doc; I'll name it for what it is, a disease! It's progressive and will eventually wipe me out slick as a whistle!"

The young neurologist saw the futility of qualifying his prognosis, so, taking a cue from Strutt's mannerism, he grabbed a prescription pad and scribbled down a medication which he hoped might prove the lady wrong. On her way to the car, Elzora used the prescription slip to press a

wad of chewing gum into, then casually tossed it into the street. In rebuffing medical help, Elzora often found herself depleted of dopamine, every neuron's friend, and so, unable to control tremors in her left arm, which now and again convulsed so frenetically she resembled a Zulu warrior at full run, Elzora would flail the air in an assault against any target unfortunate enough to wander into her path. Little wonder neighborhood teenagers named her "Elzora the Slasher." One cheeky moppet even suggested she was really "Zorro in drag."

P.J. Strutt, the couple's lumpish daughter, seemed more like a billboard picture than a vibrant, breathing person. Her inert behavior could easily persuade one that swarms of tsetse flies soared overhead, making sure that their victim functioned just shy of a coma. P.J.'s initials provoked considerable parish speculation. The parents insisted that they just never got around to naming their offspring, emphasizing that "P.J." said it all, and that they were content to add no embellishment to this Spartan signature. Others, focusing on the daughter's singular deprivation of any endowments, were convinced that P.J. stood for "Plain Jane" Strutt. This inventive sleuthing won a wide colony of adherents, who, even to the girl's frozen face, would salute her with "How are things going, Plain Jane? We haven't seen you around much, Plain Jane. We thought you might have shuffled off to the cemetery without so much as a plain hand wave."

A smaller, but no less fervent knot of "Strutt Watchers," conceding that the "Plain Jane"

appellation enjoyed plausibility, nevertheless, maintained that the initials stood "fitting and proper" for Pajamas. This opinion, lacking the sagacity of the other school, made up for its erudition by homey common sense, which was based on neighbors rarely seeing P.J. out of her nightgown, even when she tagged along with her folks to the supermarket. The owner of the adjacent Waterbeds Galore Store maintained that "Pajamas Strutt was worth fifty thousand a year in free advertisement!" Whatever the viewpoint, it was clear to all that long before formulation of the Epstein-Barr Syndrome, the contemporary yuppie malaise, P.J. was undeniably a pioneer in the phenomenon and deserved credit for profiling it.

How Amos Drogo Strutt received his clerical call will forever remain a mystery, a closely guarded Elysium secret. One thing was sure; there never appeared a time from infancy on that Amos was not dazzled, indeed thunderstruck, by money. Boss Strutt, occasionally favoring little Amos with a glance towards his crib, would explode: "Great Gawd, that happy little porker does nothing all day but draw dollar signs with his toes! Look at him giggle at the fortune he's raked in today. Someday, Boy, they'll be real dollars, and you can use your feet to fetch them, not just sketch 'em." Boss would then wrench a dollar bill from his pocket and wag it before the beaming babe. "Just look at those beady eyes glisten will yah! Yes Sir, we've got a budding banker here!" The tot's flailing hands struggled to seize the prize. Not until the child wailed in frustration did the father abandon his playfulness.

It was intriguing, as Amos grew, to observe how a dollar fixation grew with him. Nuns, who taught him in his formative years, marveled at his imagination as it transformed the most prosaic objects into symbols of currency and coinage. It was mind boggling, on picnic outings, to hear him blurt out, "Look, look at that cloud formation . . . deposit bag, bulging with silver!"

At other times, he sleuthed out bills of many denominations, deciphered in blackboard assignments, graphs, and maps. "Sure 'nuf, there's Jefferson's face staring enviously at that twenty!" And he gushed, "Take a look at old Ben Franklin drooling over those hundreds!" The Holy Names Sisters, a teaching order of considerable repute, aware of his eccentric moments, wrote them off as ramblings of a "hyper-sensitive child who would eventually grow out" of such juvenile tangents.

On occasions of birthdays or Christmas, the family, early, learned to torment Amos by packaging the only "acceptable" gift, money, in boxes, leading a crestfallen lad to believe someone was callous enough to purchase shorts or a shirt as a sick token of affection and remembrance. Everyone chuckled observing the young man's near ecstasy, as cash, a sign of "genuine love," was discovered tucked away in the bottom of each package.

Gossip, like a rusty anchor chain, rattled and grated through the county, when Amos Strutt declared his intent to enter the seminary, preparatory to serving as a priest in the diocese. It moaned and ached like the annual ice breakup of

the Snake River when, seven years later, Amos actually made it to ordination and received as his first assignment a poor barrio parish on the city's east side.

From the beginning of his ministry, though he tried in his maladroit way to mask his disgust for these "social wretches," he still showed the aloofness, if not hostility, of a grandee towards indigent peons who comprised most of his flock. These "black sheep" were not slow to sense their shepherd's bias, and so, a war zone was soon created, pitted and scarred, if not always smoldering.

Father Amos, outrageously espoused that the sole key to saving these "dregs" from paradisal boycott was to mulct them out of their last peso -- a kind of test of their "apostolic fervor." His "theology" invariably reached its summation in a notorious homily which formed part of the diocese's lore: "Wretched of God, Our Father's chosen stepchildren. You owe it to your Maker to show Him you are good sports and bear no grudges for your lamentable condition; that you acknow-ledge, in justice, your Heavenly Father could subject you to much more abandonment. But no, the Good Shepherd has generously nixed punishing you more. To be sure, your impoverish-ment speaks of a Father's alienation, but, despite this, if each sorry soul will fork over -- er -- proffer to me, a special representative of Holy Mother Church, more of his earthly goods, doubtlessly squirreled away in closet and cupboard, some mitigation of Yahweh's aversion to all that's 'polyester' in you may be expected. As with

Nineveh, the Lord will turn away from punitive designs, and you will be guaranteed a modest nook in God's 'Rancho Grande,' without fear of being 'intercepted' at the 'border' and sent packing!" Amos paused at the hint of "border agents," raked his perplexed audience, and glowered like a southern sheriff countermanded from making a consoling arrest.

To no one's surprise but his, the flood of demanded funds, which Father Strutt presumed would surge in like water down a Seattle street drain, was not forthcoming. A denigrated group can vote with its feet, to be sure, but Amos' sour parishioners voted with their hands, sitting on them when the time came to tender basic parish support at the Mass Offertory.

Amos' resources diminished, but his esurience did not. He, in many sleepless nights, cast about for the key to harvesting more money. First, he sponsored sundry gaudily designed greeting cards, with a religious message as subtle as Rambo on a rampage, a pastiche which included Mother's Day, Pour Souls' Day, Secretary's Day, My Boss's Day, and even "Have you Given your Pet a Hug?" Day. These kept a squadron of muted volunteers busy stuffing envelopes, stacking them in proper zones for cheap mailing, and carting them to the central post office who welcomed the business, whatever its meretricious motives. The whole enterprise became known as "Strutt's Dead End." The project suffered an early demise, so Amos, on a more visceral level and despite his distaste for Mexican food, customs, and dress, forced himself to propose and sponsor "Puerto Vallarta Nite," never

dreaming that this title connoted little or nothing to his congregation, most of whom couldn't afford to drive through the place, much less spend a night there, in Lucullan luxury.

Parish cash continued at a trickle like sluggish blood flow checkmated by wads of stubborn cholesterol. The pitiful clinking of coinage isolated in the collection basket baffled Strutt, who reverted once again to sketching dollar bills in the air with his toes, while fitfully tossing in bed. He grew desperate for the crinkle of greenbacks.

He now saw not monetary symbols in cloud formations, wood patterns, and floral clusters, but only menacing billows, scarred elms, and allergy-breeding milkweed. Then a light! "Of course! There's always Lotto!" he crowed. Hearing the words, he cinched his plan. Strutt was aware of some well publicized "instant millionaire" tales, divulging how one lone lottery ticket routed swarms of rivals; in fact, within his parish, one such conquest fell to a member of his flock, but before Strutt could rush to the victor and claim a share of the spoils, the parishioner, more fleet of foot, now that he could afford NIKE JOGGERS, fled his seedy surroundings to sunny suburban shores, where even the mosquitoes comported themselves with gentility. Here, the winner ingratiated himself to cautious neighbors, buzzing of his "shameful origins." He assumed the role as lead donor for a new church and, more import- antly, as the "best damn cocktail host in the neighborhood."

Strutt seemed so fixed on emerging a lotto icon he believed he could infallibly determine the

weekly outcome if he inundated the game with thousands of tickets. Desperation lulled him into dancing through fantasyland, losing himself in illusions of high finance. He massaged his ego by elevating himself to the zenith of clerical and secular status, where reputation was aglow and respect afire, like the eternal flame in Arlington Cemetery.

There would be no stopping his Titan reach for the world of prestige: "Why, I could be in line for a bishopric, even a red hat," he recklessly prattled. And again, instinctively, each night, upon retiring, he continued, as one possessed, to draw dollars with his toes. Faster and faster, until his feet ached, he sketched currency while the atmosphere grew turbid with cash. Finally, Amos lapsed into a fitful slumber; in that zone he heard his legs plead their ache and his strained toes nag rebelliously against this pecuniary regimen.

Then the solemn, sometimes malign, world of reality shook Amos' reverie, reminding him that much "seed money" would be needed to implement his "surefire" gambit. "Your Grace" plundered his mind attempting to shake loose creative ideas to enlist support. Since the Church Offertory collection was so bulimic, he dispensed with any plan to "borrow" from that larder, nor was any revenue forthcoming from his ludicrous scheme involving commemorative cards; the Puerto Vallarta debacle was not even considered; it barely got airborne before "wind shear" destroyed it.

It was in the middle of the night, despite Halcion's best efforts to shroud Strutt in slumber, that he awakened with a start. "That's it!" he

blurted "Perfect! Some quick cash! With it, I can buy 30,000 lotto tickets, corner the market, and inevitably emerge a winner!" The flummery involved the bishop's forged signature on purloined episcopal stationery and an overly accommodating banker, whose low interest loan for fifteen thousand dollars was granted to "Father Amos Strutt, whose bishop will provide one-half the collateral," the rest will derive from the spurious proposal to launch a "matching drive for fifteen thousand" among his skeptical flock. The target of the matching proposal was key to breaking down parish hostility and breaking open their wallets. This coaxer, "A tactic" rejoiced the pastor, "that never fails to warm the most wintry heart," lay in the announcement of a proposed children's playground, "with all the beeps and whistles," and a "full complement of equipment, equal to any 'normal parish.'" Amos seemed obtuse to the slam at his "abnormal" congregation, consumed as he was with his strategy. He reasoned, "This expenditure is a mere dimple compared to the canyons of riches I'll shortly be enjoying. My winnings will probably soar to several million by the next drawing," he burbled.

For the first time in his long "incarceration" among "God's stepchildren," Amos perceived a genuine interest, a driblet of enthusiasm and support. His intuition was not truant; when the matching funds' collection was taken, these simple folk, always looking to make some dent in the hostile surroundings infecting their children, proved more than generous; the fifteen thousand dollar goal was easily reached and proudly

presented to the redoubtable pastor. The chairman of the steering committee eagerly told Strutt, "We have done our part. Now we await your matching 'donation'. What an occasion for a fiesta will our playground be!"

Amos greeted these words but didn't permit them to pay a protracted visit. To himself, he groused, "It's none of their business what I do with MY money; in fact, as soon as I get my hands on those millions, I'll even build the little apes their precious playground, with lots of bars to swing on and plenty of bananas to munch. What's a paltry thirty thousand against a sweepstakes? That's mere 'chump change.'"

Plans marched in step; all that remained was purchase of 30,000 lotto tickets, which Strutt bought at the lotto's main office. "See you next week to collect on the lucky numbers," he breezily saluted the incredulous clerk as he floated out of the room. The woman ransacked her brain trying to recall who this "reverent" looked like. "Why, he's the spitting image of Ben Franklin, bald head and all!" she crowed. Just to make sure, she removed a hundred dollar bill from her cash drawer, gazed at it, and was somewhat startled. The image's face, occasionally, seemed to tilt and gazed pixilated into her eyes. "Why . . . the mouth . . . has a smirk on it, a thin slit turning up at one end." Shivers played tag up and down the lattice of her spine. Agitated, she shoved the bill into its tray, slammed the drawer, and tested its lock.

"It's been a long day," she muttered. "This all comes from handling lucre too long. It encourages idiocy."

Five days until the Saturday drawing shuffled along as sluggish as rush-hour traffic. Concentration on parish business was out of the question. Sleep impossible. Eating too, which "Your Grace" had turned into a kind of "sacrament," no longer dominated his waking hours. Amos noted how small, sloe-colored troughs of skin sagged under each eyelid, tiny curds that wriggled with each blink. He also had developed sporadic quivers around the mouth, mini tremors that darted across his face as if teased by a miniature cattle prod.

When Saturday did arrive, a perplexing atmosphere shrouded it; the day almost seemed to revel in its ancient, ambiguous reputation: gloomy on one hand, yet festive on the other. The pastor, swaggering with high hopes, observed none of this. "It's been a long pilgrimage, and now, success is just a twinkle away." "Your Grace" thought it wise not to make a personal appearance at the T.V. station where the winning numbers were to be read out; instead, with considerable discipline, he chose to watch his "sure win" in the sterile isolation of the rectory, where "news of it were best kept mute." The priest fleetingly reflected on the irony of stowing his soon-to-be good news under wraps.

"So, fame and fortune must be matched by privacy! Pure torture! Well, the award will compensate for any isolation. There's a mountain of joy in at least MY knowing what I have achieved," he confided to his audience of one.

Presuming an inevitable happy ending, Amos heard the fatuous announcer interrupt the popular

Wheel of Fortune to divulge the winning combination of seven selections which, the announcer gushed, "Could make someone out there a richer person by four million dollars!" Strutt, whose piety was as substantial as meringue, had selected his "sure fire" COMBINATIONS based on a convoluted theology: for example, A-12 was chosen for the twelve apostles; N-2 spoke of Christ's two natures; P-3 suggested the three persons in God; J-5 revealed the five joyful mysteries of the rosary; D-7 allied with the seven deadly sins; C-4 pointed to the four cardinal virtues; finally, T-10 reflected Strutt's advertence to the Ten Commandments. His selections, based on a "Baskin-Robbins" pick and choose principle, were calculated to demonstrate a "healthy" kinship to God and His Church. He nattered, "Surely my choices are all spiritually rooted, and so, I'm guaranteed success! There's no substitute for alliance with the Father. No way will God leave me euchred out of my due!" To test this silly devotion, N-2 tumbled first out of the lottery cage.

The voice of the announcer had a hollow timbre to it, as if it were emanating from a vat of soapsuds; it reverberated and echoed, mimicking itself, only to sink into an unsettling silence. T-10 followed, pursued by C-4 and A-12. Amos began to feel sweat trickle down the wattle of his neck, seep under his collar, and disperse into the forest on his chest. "Three more. Only three more," he rasped. As if to oblige him, P-3 and J-5 made their appearance. The announcer, with flair, fidgeted with the last number as it hopped out of the container. Strutt felt the man's eyes perforate him

as he strained, "D-Zero!! If anyone out there has any combination of these numbers, upon providing proof, he will leave a rich man, an envied sinner -- er pardon me -- winner! One of the 'Chosen People.'"

"Your Grace," almost in a mummified condition, spluttered, "But . . . but . . . but there are SEVEN deadly sins. Seven! Not zero! There's pride, lust, envy, anger, greed . . . ." Strutt never finished the list. He seemed to have gagged on the word "greed" and slumped forward.

"He doubtlessly strangled on something," the young coroner opined. "Yes, but there's no food or drink in sight," retorted the baffled detective. "And the feet . . . stiff as a board and sticking straight up . . . even the toes stretching for something. It beats all! Not a mark on him, yet he seems to have been grievously wounded."

Saint Jude's Hearing Aid
A Spattering of Meringue

When the postal jeep, beaming like a stubby pageant float, merrily coasted up to her mailbox, Myrna Gallera inexplicably shivered and felt that something special lay in wait. From the kitchen window of her modest home, she anxiously peered at Val Ottway who fed the battered aluminum hut with letters and advertisements, all the time chiding "Bristles," Myrna's vigilant spaniel. The carrier then puttered to his next stop, the Delbert's. When she regained composure, Myrna noticed her stiff pie meringue had leapt from its bowl, trapped in the giddy whirl of the eggbeater, which waved idly in her hand, spattering the wall with a rash of white pimples.

"*Santa Giuda, prega per me,*" she muttered; mindless of why in a whisper, she invoked the good services of the patron for hopeless causes.

Hastily wiping her hands on an apron, a frayed veteran of many kitchen skirmishes, the reedy-legged widow scurried from the room and hobbled across the lawn, nudging "Bristles" aside, to retrieve the afternoon post. It was not until she was ensconced in the dining nook that she scrutinized the delivery. Especially did the linen envelope, elegantly embossed, with a meticulously typed script, seize her attention.

"The T.C. Blaisdel Company, Certified Contest Judges?" queried Myrna. Using her thumb nail like a serrated blade against the lip of the

envelope, she fumbled for a document, scanned its message in disbelief, feverishly re-read it, gawked again at the Firm's name, and finally stared in stupor at the meringue-dabbled wall.

"A winner? A winner! Me?" she gasped. "One million dollars after matching my entrance number! *Mio Dio. Caro Giuda.* You didn't fail me. After all these years . . . I'm rich . . . ricco. . . Happy, happy life, at last!" She crooned deliriously.

When she routinely submitted the entry coupon for the "Super Sweepstakes" some six months earlier, scarcely did Myrna believe that its outrageous odds would surrender at her door, crowning her undisputed winner, upon forwarding the certified number which had accompanied the original form.

"Oh, the clothes I'll buy -- all Cassini's and Gucci's. The places I'll visit, including those smug relatives in Lucca and bella Firenze," she raptured, squeezing each elbow. Then, a menacing shift: the medusa very much alive: "Also vengeance! *La mia vendetta*, you slut, *puttana*! A lifetime of shame . . . Now my turn!"

It must be said that the marriage between Myrna and Alesandro Briccone was as turbulent as an Italian soccer game in overtime. The husband, Alesandro, was well named. As his Greek predecessor, Alexander the Great, cast a roving eye over troupes of female beauties, so Myrna's deceased husband was voracious, consumed especially in his sunset years with Luisa Alletare.

She it was, "haughty *cagna*," who heaped crimson disgrace on the unlucky widow. Myrna still remembered her rival's complacent expression as she stood on the periphery of mourners while Alesandro was permanently lowered into the "same dirt which he rolled in when alive." No wonder then, before the sod roots which covered him began to grip the soil, that Myrna changed her name back to that of her unsullied family.

Scurrying from the kitchen to the living room, she excitedly tugged at the buffet's right top drawer, where receipts, bills, correspondence, and coupons for everything from Saran Wrap to Listerine were kept. In thirty-five years, no attempt had ever been made to systemize contents. As if pleased with its carefree status, this truant pile invariably cooperated to effect smooth household management: no accounts miscalculated, no "final notices" from nervous retailers, no birthdays ignored. Rummaging through these elusive slips, Myrna intently tried to visualize the corroborative ticket with its all-important number.

"It has to be here," she rattled. "It's the only place!"

Soon, panic began pounding and her fingers knotted, spilling paper, like confetti, upon the carpet. "There is no other place . . . no other place," the staccato echoed. A frenetic, almost desperate, seizure grew insistent when the third and fourth search revealed nothing. Myrna's face flushed and sagged. Her shoulders arced. One shoe had even twisted off, forcing the woman's slight frame to list comically.

"Please come to my aid, *Santa Giuda*," croaked Myrna Gallera, whose throat, constricted like a clogged straw, trapped and plugged her initial sobs. Suddenly, a malign realization exploded, smothering one frustration with another: "HE'S got it!! The wallet . . . Alesandro. I remember his words: 'I'll keep the stub safe,' he insisted. Oh, yes it's safe, Imbecile! Idiota! I wanted to be rid of every revolting trace of him, so I rashly, stupidly, buried the wallet too. I told the mortician: 'Bury it all!' 'No more manipulation; no more deceit,' I swore. Now his insolent corpse smirks at me even from the grave!"

In his eighteen years as municipal judge, Marion Taylor Landerly had never weighed a more bizarre request from the County Coroner. His Honor, a stolid figure, who resembled Michangelo's Moses, was a fiercely committed conservative who could be relied upon, as faithfully as a bear's hibernation, to champion an individual's rights over "man-eating bureaucracy." Any government, to Landerly, larger than the local P.T.A., was suspect at the best and treasonous at worst. In a word, he could be counted on to smile favorably upon those huddled masses intimidated by City Hall with its tangle of laws and regulations, designed, in his oft quoted expostulation, "To immobilize private enterprise, ravage personal initiative, and endanger the Republican Party!"

It was fortuitous, therefore, that Myrna Gallera's request lay before his Honor's indulgent gaze as he pondered its disposition. Myrna's callow attorney, following the Coroner, explained

the urgency of the matter to the judge: "This, Your Honor, as you know, is the rainy season. Moisture makes access easier, but . . . er . . . of course, decomposition . . . of everything . . . uh . . . you catch my drift . . . is also accelerated." He darted unsteadily ahead: "This poor woman's honorable livelihood depends on your generous decision to exhume. Now we know the restrictive wisdom behind the county ordinance, regarding easy access to a stif . . . er . . . corp . . . a deceased citizen's privacy. God knows, each deserves the right to slumber; however, this matter is extraordinary. Further, I submit that this widow's beloved spouse would be distressed to know . . . uh, if he could . . . that he holds the key to her future happiness in his coat pocket, but he is impotent . . . I mean, unable to do anything about it."

No sooner did the magistrate absorb the words "Restrictive wisdom behind the county ordinance," than his mind snapped shut with the finality of a submarine hatch. He expansively determined that the aggrieved widow had every right to interrupt her husband's repose, to recover his wallet and its invaluable contents.

Myrna wisely opted to delegate her lawyer to represent her at the exhumation, though not without some emotional conflict; briefly, her terror won its struggle over curiosity. Though she harbored little doubt that Alesandro would offer no resistance, she could never have conceived what results shovel and spade would ultimately turn up.

"To my dying day, I'll never forget that miasma and the slit trace of a smile on his collapsed features," shuddered the attorney. His shaken

reaction was ratified by the seasoned coroner:
"Yes, a kind of unsettling 'Mona Lisa' crease, as if
he knew all along that our search was only a tease,
a perverse game."

Though the two witnesses suppressed their
eerie observations, out of delicacy, when they
handed the sodden wallet to the waiting widow,
her own reaction, upon opening it, was no less
disquieting. Each perceived a grim resignation
invade her features, as if ironed on like a decal.
Her eyes grew baleful and her lips compressed so
tight that they resembled a pink sliver behind
which, one could only surmise, quivered a mouth.

"Sorry, Mrs. Briccone . . . I mean, Mrs. Gallera,"
muttered her lawyer. "The only item we found in
the wallet was this smeared address and phone
number. Oddly, personal items were missing,
including the sweepstakes stub. You seemed so
sure, and we are positive the mortician honored
your request. It's almost as if your husband
deliberately disposed of its contents."

"Of course," stammered Myrna, "I completely
understand. Before he died, I trust that my
husband threw the ticket away. It isn't the first
time he impetuously discarded things, even those
of value. This address and number represent
nothing of worth, of that I am sure."

Following the two officials' retreat, Myrna
collapsed like a wicker bag onto the couch, still
fingering the scrawled address rescued from the
wallet. Two veins, like ganglia, rototilled around
her temple. She raked the note savagely with her
glance. "The last memento is it? This address . . .
HERS . . . Your final gift to me?" she spluttered. "I

know it! You gave my prize to that *strega*, that witch . . . a final love token . . . a beautiful *pegna d'amore* from her passionate lover. Well, I have my own pledge to make."

Luisa Alletare was perplexed, curious, if not a bit wary, to receive a call from Myrna Briccone. She had never met the woman, naturally, and had little appetite for it. After all, she quite understood the chilling hatred which must still scratch at her rival's heart. Were she the loser, defeat would probably be as acrid. However, Luisa no longer celebrated a triumph: "Who can boast when the race is finished and the prize won?" The widow seemed anxious to meet her; indeed, Luisa detected an urgency in her voice, at once crisp, yet civil.

"Why not?" Luisa mused. "The past ultimately is written in lemon juice. Just possibly, all rage was spent with Alesandro's death." So, though reserved, Luisa consented to a meeting, the following afternoon. "Why not at Saint Jude's?" she probed. "This, I believe, is the parish for us both, and I stroll there nearly every day." Myrna hastily agreed to the rendezvous, keenly aware that the suggested site converged on the precinct of her favorite patron; St. Jude's intercessory powers she clamored for more than at any time in her turbulent life.

Each woman slept fitfully that night. Myrna especially lay contorted, as if snagged in a roomful of yarn. She arose, stalked through her house, massaging the award letter requesting a prompt response. Desperate, she knew what was required.

Confrontation was a must; she would demand what was rightfully hers. Failing in this, she had nothing to lose. A final reversal would only be a ludicrous epilogue to her life's tragedy. But hers would not conclude as the only unhappy drama. Luisa too, ironically, with the help of Alesandro's gun, would play out her dénouement.

On the following afternoon, when the two met, each greeted the other with stiff politeness. Luisa knew immediately that their meeting was to be more than a fugitive encounter, a perfunctory postscript to a love plot each had a hand in writing years before. Myrna archly spoke:
"You have some personal effects of my husband's. These I want. They belong to me all of them. I have a perfect right to everything."

"Everything? Alesandro was never totally yours, far from it! So why wildly suggest all is owed to you? Some of his precious keepsakes I will never give up."

"'Precious keepsakes'?" chortled Myrna. "I'm not talking about a fortune, not from Alesandro, an unproductive fool! I'm referring only to some small mementoes, like his wallet and its personal contents which he squeezed into your hands before he died."

Luisa, equally aloof, snapped: "The wallet's contents? Yes, I have them, and other tokens of affection as well. Your sentimentality for a few souvenirs perplexes me, but this I'll do: I'll bring his 'personal effects,' as you warmly refer to them, all of them, here tomorrow and give you your fair share. You see, I hold no grudges. Why should I?

Perhaps, only pity, because you were a wife to one who wanted to live in more than a desert."

The following afternoon, a radiantly clear one for winter, found the two women again in front of Saint Jude's Church. Luisa, buoyant, handed Myrna the elusive packet of contents from Alesandro's wallet. As relieved as she was bewildered with this gesture so foreign to her expectations, the flustered woman seized it, nervously rubbing the sweepstake's stub as she would a talisman.

"Your winning ticket, of course. Yes, word spreads fast whether news be good or bad. Congratulations. I wish you every happiness."

Unable to interpret this generous scenario, Mryna remained mutely captive, as if studying a Greek riddle. She mumbled a sterile "thank-you" to the source of her grief. "I didn't expect this . . . I didn't . . . ." Her voice trailed away like a lost radio beam.

"Surprised?" asked Luisa. "Why, six years ago I, too, won a sweepstakes. It's a miraculous feeling! You shouldn't be denied." Then, before Myrna could decipher a clue to this puzzle, Luisa brightened: "Let's go in now and pay a visit to Jude!"

Numb, even questioning the stability of the person in front of her, Myrna turned to indulge this eccentric proposal, construing it as a kind of pious finale to a distasteful plot.

Entering the church and inching her way to the side chapel, where the Saint's shrine cast spears of hushed shadows between the glow of mischievous vigil candles, Myrna suddenly stumbled in dismay.

There, sitting quietly in a pew, a handsome, dark-haired lad of about six smiled contagiously at her, much the same way that Alesandro, in younger, halcyon days, radiated happiness before it became clear that she would bear him no children, that their union was as insubstantial as meringue.

Myrna froze, suddenly enervated, drained of life. She shuffled unsteadily towards the fresh vision before her and reached for his outstretched hand.

"This is Jude," beamed his mother. "We named him after our Saint, who heard our prayer." Then, without a word, Luisa clasped her son's hand; with his other, he waved first in the direction of the benign patron of hopeless causes, then to Myrna, whose eyes flooded, blurred, and lost all focus.

Saint Dympna's Therapy
Getting to Know You

From a distance it looked like a huge weather sock, black, with rivulets of red and a spangling of gold. But closer viewing exposed the macabre truth. Left stranded in the breeze, hanging from a branch of an apple tree, the corpse of His Excellency, the Most Reverend Carleton Matthias Spingarn, dangled helplessly before the invasive stare of passers-by. His black soutane, fringed with red piping, contrasted morbidly with the victim's gold pectoral cross and chain, which had been cinched around his neck then coiled about a sturdy limb. Whoever orchestrated this lurid drama was not without mirth for, propped against the tree, was a well-thumbed copy of Willa Cather's, *Death Comes for the Archbishop.* Whether the breeze had colluded with the assailant or the act was intentional, the novel la open to a page which piqued the attention of sleuths who rushed to the bizarre scene in hopes o making some sense of it all.

"No accident this. Cather's novel has been placed here with more than theatre in mind; some clue snickers at us in these pages, defying unraveling," murmured inspector Willard K. Jansens as he scanned the book's engaging style. Meanwhile, word of the outrage sprinted from door to door, mingling with gossip, wild speculations, and salacious conclusions of dubious validity. The Archbishop's chancery was, of course, among the

first offices alerted. Fortunately, the recently appointed auxiliary bishop, Dustin Urban Deluso, was at his desk when the secretary, exultant with breathlessly throbbing information which this young "Episcopal upstart" was ignorant of, blurted, "Oh, what's it all coming to? How could anyone have invaded the Archbishop's quarters, killed his Excellency, carried his Excellency to the garden and there suspended his Excellency like a Christmas ornament?" Bishop Deluso, no ally of Irene Lacey, the burbling secretary whom he had long considered dotty over his deceased predecessor and blind to his several faults, coolly nodded in the direction of the wailing devotee. He was aware that in no way would he be able to mute her plangent posturing, which, as he put it, "would have to run its course like a pesty head cold."

Deluso, in other contexts, dropping his frosty demeanor, registered shock, anger, and grief over this sacrilege. Though he would never forgive the quarantine which Spingarn threw around him, recommending that he be made an "auxiliary" instead of a "coadjutor" bishop, thereby depriving him of the right to succession, he did allow that the archbishop deserved a better send-off. Deluso confided to his circle of friends, "For one who had an aversion to displays, the 'Spinner' must be appalled at this vulgar mime of his final exit."

Dustin Deluso was a local boy, born of Italian-American parents of the second generation, who still cling to the Bocca Toscana of their native Siena; still make their own vino roso from black Muscat grapes whose slips had been smuggled into the country by their parents; still celebrate

holidays, including christenings, with caravans of pasta, salads, a bewildering assortment of breads, formaggio, especially Gorgonzola Senese, and, of course, sweets tipsy with brandy from coveted desserts unique to Assisi's Perugia. Beyond cultivating a fastidious taste for Italian food and drink, Bishop Dustin Deluso, while still a callow seminarian, appropriated an equally important "inheritance," namely, a good dose of "furberia," a shrewdness or cunning, which consistently found him in the right place at the right time, mouthing the right responses and formulating flattering questions. No wonder contemporaries saluted him, in apparent good jest, as "L'Olivo," acknowledging his unctuous composure and oiled rhetoric.

Endowed with a keen mind and the eloquence to express its contents, Dustin had been favored to do his theology studies abroad, in Belgium, at the prestigious University of Louvain. Here he met and became close friends with a native Belgian, Jan Vandeputte, who, lacking Dustin's acumen, compensated for it by a sunny, disarming personality and a fierce loyalty to his friends. Some construed this as blind hero-worship. Jan lightly brushed aside this accusation of excessive allegiance as a "family trait," evinced by his twin brother who certainly shared the same virtues. The deceased Archbishop, very much alive at the time, sponsored Dustin's higher education; he was accustomed to refer to him as "Our Laser Lord," descrying in the young scholar an outstanding shepherd the diocese could inchoately be proud of. Deluso, despite his benefactor's known conservatism and generosity, indiscriminately, but

always cautiously, adopted the most liberal views of some professors; he was consumed by Vatican II theology which the Archbishop never entirely "bought." In the presence of his close associates Deluso strained to espouse what he thought were "cutting edge" contentions: women in the priesthood; a trimming of papal authority; general confession; Christ's belated awareness of his divine mission. These and other "trendy vapors," as Spingarn dismissed them, never failed to evoke, however guardedly, the most ardent salvos of approval from Deluso. He righteously brushed aside, in a most illiberal fashion, any "truant" who might mumble a reservation or two about his radical left-wing sentiments. His was a gnostic world, an arcanum whose "mysteries" only a few "luminaries" may access.

Despite digging a potential chasm between himself and the Archbishop, as a student, and later, as ordained priest, and finally bishop, Deluso never comported himself as anyone but a respectable conservative, invariably supporting the "proven forms" and ostensibly protecting hallowed traditions with the firmness of a truss stabilizing a feisty hernia. He was convinced that the senior clergy, including the Archbishop, were left none the wiser about his real convictions after they weighed his words and took his political pulse. In a word, the young opportunist told the Archbishop and his conservative cadre exactly what each wanted to hear, while not betraying his true convictions to any except intimate friends like Jan Vandeputte who occasionally visited America to reaffirm their esteem. To Jan, all theology was

frivolous, like any game, not to be taken too seriously, and certainly nothing to brew antagonisms over. He never saw "Janus" in the face of his American friend; never interpreted his duplicity as anything but cleverness.

But Archbishop Spingarn was not as addled as some believed, or hoped, at any rate. While not dazzled by the sparkle many associated with every Vatican II nugget, he remained obedient to the Council, exercising a wary acceptance of its teachings, but never camouflaging his misgivings. Some clerical seers, like a troupe of noisy dervishes, harangued the Archbishop for his foot-dragging in implementing liturgical decrees, but none could question his pastoral insight which persuaded him to go slow when the only jittery option for a liturgical celebration was, as he described it, a variation on "a shabby tent revival," adding, "These aberrations are cranked out by 'experts' who cannot dance, sing, compose, or intelligently read literature beyond a boy scout manual." The old man would sometimes grouse: "Everyone and his dog lays claim these days to being an 'artist,' solely because some poor dupe can traipse aimlessly about a sanctuary without falling on his butt; pluck sleepily at a guitar string that would rush Tex Ritter to intensive care; and rasp out a desultory tune with the 'mellow resonance' of a furniture auctioneer. That isn't liturgy! That's nightclub antics and damned poor ones at that!" Finishing one of his polemics, the Archbishop would fix a twinkling gaze on his protégé and seemed to savor the masked discomfort he glimpsed there. "Yes," he would silently chortle,

"You will make a fine 'auxiliary': traveling the diocese, confirming the laity in their faith, and occasionally dedicating a church. Yes, indeed, there's enough work out there to keep you from thinking too much."

About fifty miles northeast of Louvain lies the inviting town of Gheel, whose patron is Saint Dympna, an early martyr, who had dedicated her life nursing the mentally ill. The discovery of her grave in the 13th century kindled the town's devotion to their patron, and to this day inspires folk to welcome into their homes one or two mentally handicapped souls, lavishing on them all the attention and love of family. Further, a large sanatorium dominates the skyline, its wings arcing to embrace everyone, whatever their condition or status.

Several years earlier two young seminarians, like pilgrims, reached the outskirts of Gheel. Dustin Deluso and Jan Vandeputte, as part of their pastoral curriculum, had been assigned to work in the hospital a month among the mentally ill. Gazing down on the town, cuddled next to protective hills and hushed forests of spruce and shimmering aspen, travelers invariably feel the nurturing presence of the village's patroness whose venerated example blurs, if not nullifies, the cozy distinction between the sick and the sane. In this irenic setting such glib divisions are ludicrous; a mysterious and salutary reciprocity between patient and nurse accentuates humanity's common blight and frailty. "Come to think of it, we're all slightly daft and just a little off plumb," chirped Jan, without appreciating the truth behind his

cheery insight. "Some have simply profiled it a bit more," he concluded, as he and the bishop reminisced on that zealous and happy time of relative innocence.

With the sordid murder still mutilating his memory, Deluso almost histrionically moaned, "At times I wonder if life isn't the perpetuation of one vast mistake? We all seem snagged in a distinctive madness! It would be the stuff of miracles to make a nostalgic visit to Gheel, a pilgrimage long overdue, to Saint Dympna's home. All folks are fortified in the wondrous harmony that orchestrates everything there. Perhaps some few, older friends and veteran residents, will remember me and stiffen my faith." Jan rejoined: "Well, one whom you knew best, Dustin, an American woman, whose husband was Belgian, is no longer a resident at Dympna's. Since her insanity was judged incurable, and her husband deceased, a son took her back to America to be close to her. Surely you recall her lamentable state, strafed by religious scruples -- an obsession to obey Church law blindly and refusal to put the slightest tincture of humane interpretation into law. Her skewed values never could accept a Lord of mercy and a Church to match! Her husband blistered the Church for her tangled condition, and his rancor knew no limits against that which, he believed, caused this 'human wreckage.'"

"Of course, I remember her. What a distortion of faith and a sorry victim of brittle authority. All vapors and fancy. I never could expel from her mind! Doctors agreed that the assault of 'doomsday religion' on her was irreversible. An

irony, I felt, for her to be named 'Killingworth'!
Myrna Killingworth! Tomorrow you return to
Belgium, Jan. Try to find out from the hospital
where, in the States, her son moved her. Since the
institutional church, ostensibly, is the occasion for
her eclipse, it should offer her solace for one motive
alone: she belongs to Saint Dympna's family, as do
we all!

Bishop Deluso was unable to decipher the
character of Inspector Jansens. He seemed the
epitome of thoroughness and discreet enough to
qualify as a Swiss banker. But, there was a
captious reserve about him, which though not
glacial, registered just above freezing. His more
than skimpy acquaintance with the Church, mixed
with a frosty aloofness, suggested that at some
period he had retreated in anger from its reach.
Undeniably, police interest in the Archbishop's
murder was intense, but the shabby mauling of the
man himself seems to have evaded Inspector
Jansen's interest; sympathy for the victim seemed
lost in chase after his assailant.

With an ambiguous smile that appeared as an
almond-shaped track across his face, Inspector
Jansens favored the auxiliary Bishop with a
glance. "I would appreciate it, Sir, if you would
study the text of the novel found at the base of the
tree which was the Archbishop's last detour. I'll
leave *Death Comes for the Archbishop* with you
this evening; perhaps in the quiet of your study
some clues may surface."

And so it happened that night, with Verdi's
Requiem playing in the background, Bishop Deluso
found himself perusing Willa Cather's literary

achievement. Particularly did he concentrate on a passage which collared his attention: "When the Archbishop dismounted to enter the church, the women threw their shawls on dusty pathway for him to walk upon, and as he passed through the kneeling congregation, men and women snatched for his hand to kiss the Episcopal ring . . . ." Deluso's eyes could not shake free of this passage.

"Why does this nag at me?" he queried, adding, "It simply describes a gesture of respect for Church authority. Cather's scenes descry a faith-filled people's love affair with God and his represent-atives." Further insight strayed from him, so he closed his concentration to everything but the measured solemnity of Verdi, whose dolorous notes conspired with the night to seal up everything in a coffin of darkness.

The Bishop drifted into a desultory sleep; his grip on the novel relaxed, and it tumbled to the floor. The thud startled him. He bolted up, alert, reddening. "That's it! Why couldn't I have seen it? The ring! The Archbishop's ring is missing. It didn't register at the time, but I remember now that his hand was bare. The killer must have wrenched the ring from his finger, then used Cather's descriptive scene as a key to the whole sordid mystery. 'Track down the ring and you will find me,' is the killer's boast. What arrogance! Bankrupt cynicism!"

"That's an interesting hypothesis, Bishop," mused Jansens. "Of course, Sir, the only way such an assumption can be validated is to find the ring and then hope to unlock the symbolism it holds for the killer. The ring might stand for

something more than a shepherd's authority over his flock, a sign more devious than first meets the eye. If that sounds credible, I suggest that the assailant was acting more like an executioner, or avenger, than a mindless murderer. So, let's keep all options open."

Days limped by, and the Auxiliary Bishop's depression began to ebb. Father Jan Vandeputte, following a few days inquiry, phoned from Belgium relaying some important information to his friend, Dustin. "Myrna Killingworth, believe it or not, three years ago, was transferred from Saint Dympna's to your own city, at the instigation of a son. I can only presume she still resides at 'Serenity Heights Convalescent Centre.' I don't know what her son's business is, but the staff there can probably clue you in."

The very next day, Dustin Deluso, strolled down the sinuous sidewalk leading to the foyer of "Serenity Heights." The landscaping was impeccable: lawns were painstakingly groomed; flowers -- dahlias, gerania, marigolds -- each rivaling the other for attention, posed grandly in manicured bays which bordered the walkway along the face of the building. In serried order, as if chaperoning these floral revelers, stood tall junipers, smartly trimmed. Oddly, dominating the center of the property, loomed a cypress tree. More at home in cemeteries, this funereal veteran served as a melancholy reproach to its happy "neighbors," reminding all who should pass by that these warm precincts are illusory and must inevitably yield to mirthless regions of wintry sleep. Gazing at the giant cypress, Bishop Deluso,

despite his worldly climb, could not help but note amidst all this flowery riot, that the last word seems conceded to death and its many faces. In a voice foreign to his own ears he stammered, "The price one pays for nuptials with material goods. What insanity we buy into."

Approaching Myrna Killingworth silhouetted in the room's muted light, Deluso genially spoke her name. She looked on him at first quizzically, then smiled brightly. "How long has it been, Father?" she asked. Then, answering her own question, whispered, "Whatever. Too long." Deluso, seating himself, studied his former acquaintance, hoping to discover some trace of healing.

"Yes, Myrna, far too long since those wonderful visits at Saint Dympna's. I hope cloudy days have been replaced by brighter skies."

Looking perplexed, Myrna calmly noted, "Oh, Saint Dympna continues to spoil me with her gifts. She has never abandoned me. Why, she brought me here, so my son could be near, and as soon as he can spare a minute -- he's frightfully busy you know -- he no doubt will drop by. I expect him any day now. Such a wonderful boy, is Willard, so unlike his father, Mr. Jansens, who was always at war with something, including his family. Quite vindictive, you know. Though I try, I'm afraid I'm not as generous and forgiving as my son. Why, he even keeps his father's name, whereas I favor my maiden name."

Then, as an afterthought, Myrna exclaimed, "Oh, I nearly forgot to show you Saint Dympna's latest present. Look at this splendid gift, another token of her affection."

Cradled in her hand was the ring of the deceased Archbishop Spingarn, sparkling with luster in a blighted world, and surprising "L'Olivo" with something more precious than any diamond -- namely, an unmistakable awareness that he too sorely needed St. Dympna's therapy.

Saint Isidore's Harvest:
Bringing in the Sheaves
Something up his Sleeve

 Grant Goodloe never looked more seraphic. He was found in his space-saver rocker as upright as a spring groundhog testing the sun. The cuff of the blood pressure gauge sagged lamely around his right arm, registering "zero." Grant's perplexing smirk, his wife concluded, could only be related to that little monitor, his constant companion, whose first optimistic readings invariably sent him into paroxysms of rage, challenging its accuracy and imputing its honesty. However, by the time that Grant savagely tore the sleeve from one arm and cinched it to the other, retesting his condition, the systolic reading, acquiescing to its owner's dire prediction, had soared, like an Apollo rocket to an alarming 190, with the diastolic trying to rival it. "Just as I thought!" he would bellow. "My pressure's rampaging out of control, and no damn machine can weasel out of the fact!" Designed to nurture health, this impish device, obliging this owner's anxiety, eventually killed him, coaxing his cerebral arteries to pop like bubble gum, stretched beyond its limit by a mischievous child.

 Just at lunch, Estelle Goodloe discovered her husband's jauntily erect corpse. She fumbled for a prayer of thanksgiving as she returned a rather pungent deviled egg sandwich to the refrigerator. Then, she clutched the phone, dialing two individuals: Monsignor Morris Bledie, Saint

Isidore's avuncular pastor, and Doctor Eldon Scurry. The latter was Grant's long-suffering cardiologist whom his former patient fulminated against once a month for his sanguine assurances that an imminent demise was merely a creature of his sulphurous fancy.

The good cleric, who had refereed many a skirmish between these two gladiators, arrived first to mediate their final separation. He perfunctorily administered the Church's Last Rites to the victim.

"Conditionally, of course, Estelle, because we can never be sure when Grant's soul bade farewell to his body."

"You can in this case, Father," rasped the widow. "I can't imagine Grant's soul wanting to stick around one minute longer than necessary!"

Then, noting her pastor's use of the word "conditional," she confided: "You gave me quite a start. At first, I thought you might be suggesting that there was a chance the poor devil would make a comeback."

"Oh no, Estelle," hastened the Monsignor. "I was merely implying that one's transition from this world may not be as instant as Sanka Coffee or Prem Cream, if you pardon the homey comparisons."

This assurance spared the priest from administering the same comforting sacrament to Estelle, whose pulse, always somewhat erratic, settled down to a contented rhythm.

As puzzling as an Internal Revenue form was how these two combatants became acquainted, engaged and eventually married. Their

association could only be described as "connubial blitz"; relentless assaults were occasionally relieved by a smoldering truce. Oddly, each seemed to thrive in this war zone, as if the only slender alternative would be a marooned exile, far from any trenches of belligerence.

Grant refused to accompany his wife anywhere: "Travel's for them that have no home," he would grunt, as if his dreary environment were modeled on Nazareth's blissful family.

His conversation, with the exception of an occasional snarl, was sparse: "A mouth's to eat with, not to gabble," he would snort. Likewise, his charm never extended to surprising his wife with a gift, unless it was some gratuitous hectoring on household management: "Money's for saving, not squandering," he would snap.

Estelle too, over the years, had learned to confront her antagonist with the brittle severity of an attack dog trainer, always alert to the jugular. Fortunately, she had consistently worked since her marriage, so was unaccountable for the clothes she purchased, meager entertainment she enjoyed, and even the modest treats she relished, apart from those staples whose expense they divided, with all the bounty of Dickens' Fagan among his apprentices.

Occasionally, Estelle, desperate, would dramatize a profound disgust with her lot. One memorable Christmas she drew a skimpy holiday decoration for her "beloved's" Spartan supper table. With lipstick, she sketched a desolate fir tree on a paper plate and embellished it with a single ornament, hanging forlornly from a spindly

limb. Finally, she fastened a plastic compass to the base, with the inscription: "A gift for the hopelessly lost." This trinket she gingerly tossed on the kitchen table, before departing to her brother's for some attempt at Christmas cheer.

Upon her return, Grant, fidgeting with his blood pressure cuff, reminded her "that it's your turn to take out the garbage." Stomping into the kitchen she discovered a festive scrawl on the sack: "Season's Greetings! Santa."

No wonder, then, that Estelle was not in need of Noah's ark to carry her safely over waves of remorse on the occasion of her husband's exit. Besides, she was to learn, astonishingly, that, despite himself, Grant was to provide her with an unparalleled White Christmas, forever transforming her life.

Grant may have been bankrupt in love, but was surprisingly resourceful in insurance. Particularly attractive was a policy which matured upon the death of either spouse. Because Estelle for years had scuffled with a vexing heart condition, exacerbated, in Doctor Scurry's opinion, "by domestic tension," the policy held an unique proviso: its dividends would be more plump on the slim chance that her husband should retreat from this world first.

Despite his challenging bouts with induced blood pressure, Garth felt confident that his wife would surely precede him into eternity; furthermore, since, in large part, he orchestrated that "domestic strife" which their physician alluded to, he estimated that he could conceivably facilitate her journey. In brief, Grant always

presumed that the "sheaves" of this premium insurance would be harvested by him and not Estelle, whose tenure in the orchard of life he viewed as ephemeral.

It was, without doubt, and with ulterior motives, that Garth casually inquired into his wife's health, resonating to words like fibrillation, infarction, and valve with all the sparkle of a lottery winner. However, the fertile grain yield fell into Estelle's lap when her husband's stroke brought her a stroke of luck: a ripe dividend of $300,000.00.

"Yes, Estelle," puffed the venerable Monsignor Bledie, through grooved cheeks which looked freshly tilled. "Though your life with Grant was not the happiest, God has now chosen to reward you with the sheaves of this earth. Husband these well, and, relying on good Saint Isidore, patron of farmers, be like the wise man of the gospel who stored up produce in seven years of plenty for seven years of famine."

Estelle, more composed than at any time in her married life, sat reflectively in the shepherd's neat but weathered rectory and absorbed his words: "I appreciate your advice, Father. Believe me, I will not squander this abundance; neither will I let it lie fallow, as that foolish man in the parable who stupidly buried his talents. This I promise, Monsignor: if the good Lord continues to favor me, I'll generously continue to help Saint Isidore's reap plenty, so our dream of a new church can finally be realized."

"We can only pray," murmured the priest. "Now, may I ask a difficult favor? On the subject

of prayer, let's not forget Grant that the Lord will shower him with much needed compassion."

"'Shower?' A deluge more likely will be required!" exclaimed the widow. "However, I'll try, Father, but only because I know the Lord's store must be enormous, even in the commodity of mercy. Still, I don't want to exhaust his supply on one poor devil."

Thus the colloquy, which followed Grant's interment, concluded, and Saint Isidore surely smiled; the seeds planted on this occasion were not scattered on barren rock, but in peculiarly fertile soil.

Weeks moped by and found a preoccupied widow thumbing through investment sources, like *Forbes* and *Fortune*, in addition to seeking fiscal advice from well-meaning friends and references. She ransacked her brain for lucrative schemes. Like Seattle rain, proposals were plentiful but none really whetted her appetite, urging her to commit her insurance bonanza to prosperous investment! Then, in the middle of one night, the answer startled her with all the insistence of a shrill smoke alarm!

"Of course!" she bolted upright, warbling her delight, "Grant would have worshiped it! A kind of substitute 'wife'! A blood pressure monitor with a reassuring voice. A loving recording to replace a dial's crisp reading. This is it! An affectionate gem, a doting partner to soothe and comfort all the 'Grants' of this world!" She rambled on excitedly: "Why, such a marvel could be modeled upon those popular new cash registers in Zelanski's supermarket, which pleasantly chime: 'Cabbage,

thirty-four cents a pound,' and 'Bumble Bee Tuna, fifty-nine cents a can!' To be sure, my voice is not as silken, but can still sweetly confide if one's blood pressure settles at normal, marginal, or dangerous levels. Think of it: a caressing nurse, a caring mother and warm lover in one embodiment of health. In fact, I'll call it 'Grant's Guardian Angel.' Even Grant could cozy up to this mate!"

Rhapsodic, Estelle bounded from bed, convinced that fate or Saint Isidore, importuned her to open her door to Fortune and invite it in.

So, after months of design, production models, marketing studies, and advertising, the miraculous gadget finally tumbled onto the shelves of several prominent outlets. The first inventory sold out in less than a month, pressing the manufacturer to double his next stock. This too was rapidly depleted, with back orders choking the computer. Soon, Estelle's creation, aptly baptized, "Grant's Guardian Angel," was found hugging the arms of a large, starved male population. These cozy monitors, variegated like a spring blouse, were rarely far from the anxious reach of husbands seeking affirmation in their health quest.

Every zealot would eagerly slip the supple sleeve over his forearm, hugging the artery, and squeeze the pump until "200" was registered; at that level, a dulcet, if not seductive, tone would intervene: "That's fine, Dear; don't squeeze too tight." The needle would then stutter downwards to sundry systolic-diastolic markings. If these ranged in the "safe zone," melodious words would coo: "Congratulations Honey! You are very 'Normal.'" Marginal case readings were no less

charmed by: "Good, Darling! But we can improve."
In those worrisome cases of hypertension, with its
alarming surges, a mellifluous accent would urge:
"Sorry, Lamb. Your reading is high. Now relax for
me!"

All in all, this solicitous "companion" exerted an
almost mystical influence over troops of frazzled
junior executives, harried taxi drivers, and
arthritic retirees, all of whom craved a supporting
hand or sleeve, in this case, to coax them through
each frenetic day. In short, their adoring interest
earned Estelle interest with each healthy bank
deposit.

Despite her acquired affluence, she did not
forget her promise to Saint Isidore. And the saint,
good husbandman that he is, must have looked
benignly on his votary, especially as he viewed his
new edifice largely brought to fruition through
Estelle's pledge.

Strangely, in the seven years of plenty that had
favored her business venture, Estelle had never
been tempted personally to toy with her wondrous
product, which so many clung to almost like a
surrogate lover. Doubtless, her disdain of the
device stemmed from memory of Grant's exclusive
fixation with blood pressure in earlier, dour days.
Furthermore, since her husband's demise and her
business triumph, bearing his name, Estelle felt
that her health problems had largely dissipated. "I
don't need a machine, even a sweet-talker, to tell
me what I already know: that my heart is as sound
as my bank account."

However, her euphoria was premature. Bleak events wriggled free from the hands of protective spirits and grinned mischievously in her direction.

Another Christmas season, the seventh after Grant's death, paid a visit like a sorcerer. A stunningly white one it was. Pillows of snow were tucked into every branch. Houses were dressed in pearl-like ruffles, their eaves sparkling in bonnets of frost. Milky strands of electric wires joined residence to residence, each plunged into a silence where every sound was outlaw.

Estelle, saddened by the season, sat subdued and exceedingly alone before the insolent glow of her fireplace, nostalgically listening to holiday music, which evoked somber, if not bitter, memories. Her eyes brimmed with tears, some hostile, as she absorbed the lyrics to "White Christmas": *I'm dreaming of a white Christmas, / Just like the ones I used to know."*

"More like nightmares," she mumbled. Unconsciously, her glance roved over some boxes containing the one "present" which had, in her ambiguous life, brought enrichment -- her cherished invention set aside as gifts for a few friends. She curiously reached for one, fondled it, and immediately, vividly, despite herself, thought of Grant. Perfunctorily, she stroked the mechanism, and, as was his ritual, slipped the talisman through her arm, secured it, squeezed the bulb permitting the arrow to climb to its proper level. Then, alarmingly, she noticed only an insignificant dip in the reading; in fact, to her horror, the arrow careened upward, straining dangerously high! Suddenly, a voice, glacial and

derisive, grated: "Too high, Estelle! Dangerous, Estelle! It can kill, Estelle! Season's Greetings . . . Daaarling!"

Like an epileptic, the needle began to convulse wildly, ruthlessly inching forward. Estelle could not shake off the strident, piping mockery, unmistakably Grant's! "Dangerous, Estelle! It's killing, Estelle! Santa says, `Season's Greetings' Daaarling . . . . "

Then, as if a dancing, electric coil were slashing at her arms and legs, she felt afire, numbness disarmed every sinew and tendon. Her head throbbed, as if a dozen truck bumpers were pounding at the walls of her skull, only to reverse, and batter them again. Her eyes, like opaque doorknobs, grotesquely protruded and revolved slowly in her head, gazing blindly around the room. Finally, the gaily colored sleeve, "Grant's Guardian Gauge," sank from her arm, its glass dial impishly reflecting the purpled face of its former owner.

She was discovered sitting primly, if not quizzically, in the same chair which earlier had witnessed her husband's departure.

Monsignor Bledie sadly celebrated the liturgical Burial Mass for Estelle Goodloe. In his brief homily, he praised her for the generous bequest which would vastly assist Saint Isidore's building fund.

"'Estelle,' you know, means 'star,'" he explained to the hushed congregation. "It is proper in this Christmas season, when we remember that wondrous star which shone over a small residence and glittered upon a Miracle, that today another

'Star' should shine over our modest house, witnessing something miraculous as well, the birth of our new church in honor of Saint Isidore, patron of plentiful harvests."

At these words, his flock nodded joyous assent, blessed themselves, and prayed, "Amen."

Saint Lawrence's Barbecue
An Eye on Votive Candles

Father Jason Crepit's fingertips played a nervous tattoo on his briefcase, conveying as much anxiety as did his voice. "Is there a second to Dr. Porphyry's motion? Is no one to second this proposal?" The Jesuit priest's hands were soft, pudgy, with dimples stippling each knuckle. These tiny creases danced in sync to the Dean's tremors which seemed to mock this veteran of academic wars, as if he were a callow novice. The "autistic" reaction of his academic council revealed their negativity both to the matter at hand and to its sponsor, Lawrence Ignatius Porphyry. Most students, working toward graduation, bullied and scourged by Porphyry, had to endure the inferno of his classes, or at least a purgatorio, before they could savor that paradisal moment when, clutching their well-earned diplomas, they fled from this nightmare.

Generations of these initiates had conferred upon their tormentor the sobriquet, "The Lip." Sundry interpreters vied to claim insight into this appellation. One school for scandal, boasting the widest currency, laid the source to Porphyry's lips which seemed permanently swollen and splayed, like stuffed cannelloni seeping at the seams. This distortion reinforced his perpetual pouting demeanor. However valid the "sulking" explanation, another group ascribed the title to "The Lip's" apodictic behavior.

"No pope," huffed a grizzled Jesuit history prof, "from the chair of Saint Peter to the present Pontiff, ever handed down such *ex cathedra* judgments with the silly certitude of Porphyry."

Another peer, a department chair, tartly observed, "Only a cretin would approach that 'cannon' without wearing a flak vest."

Though hermeneutics stumbled in discovering the definitive origin of Lawrence's nickname, his baptismal name, confided Porphyry's mother some years earlier to Father Crepit, "fitted him like a glove." She observed that her son's entry into this world involved a breach birth, presaging an early reluctance to step ashore and join the human parade.

But after considerable prodding, pulling, and coaxing, the baby's debut was successful. As its head peeped through, a generous rug of fiery red hair startled observers, igniting much chatter. Despite his exhausted mother's attempt to hush his squalling, which sounded more like an execration than whimpering, she met with little success. Moreover, the introduction to his home, en route from the hospital, was replete with drama. The mother's brother noted a ribbon of smoke curling from his car's engine which suddenly burst into flame.

Fumes invaded the chassis. Without reflecting, the driver seized the yowling bundle and effortlessly tossed the infant into some juniper shrubbery where he lay wailing like Moses in the rushes. This thicket did cushion the child's landing, but certainly didn't mitigate his irascible response to the deliverance.

No wonder then that the child's mother, whose devotion to the saints and belief in celestial "signatures" were ardent, should have scoured Butler's *Lives of the Saints* for an apt patron her son could be named after. The child's Promethean association with fire clamored for a "right choice." The decision was not long in coming. Saint Lawrence, an early Christian martyr, was revered for his unique witnessing to the Christian faith -- death by a primitive technique of "barbecuing" victims on a gridiron. He it was who jested with his tormenters, "I am done on this side; you may turn me over!" In every respect but the saint's humor the mother found a parallel between Lawrence of old and her offspring.

She exclaimed, "What a perfect model to watch over my dyspeptic darling." This was the only time any could accept the slightest affinity between the two.

Lawrence Porphyry was so seated in the college's conference room that his back was to the right side of the table, and only his profile could be scanned by colleagues on his left. He seemed to be gazing at a point beyond the focus of committee members. There was something baleful about his stare, an unblinking hostility like a lizard targeting its prey.

Porphyry's motion was as crisp as its author: "Resolved that all arts and sciences candidates, falling below a cumulative C+, notwithstanding a higher grade in the major, should be expelled from the college." As he sulphurously put it: "If those intellectual junkies in other schools tolerate such sewage, they are welcome to wallow in it."

Then, mischievously, he added, like a computer defaulted to scoff at the religious commitment of Father Crepit: "Of course, we'll have to put aside all pious pap which would misconstrue this motion as 'unloving.' Briefly, Assisi and his birds must go; Hobbes' *Leviathan* stays."

This cynical salvo prompted Dr. C. Blaine Powell, respected member of the philosophy department, peremptorily to "Call for the question." Long ago, Powell learned the futility of squandering energy by engaging Lawrence in debate.

To no surprise the motion failed nearly unanimously with the exception of Porphyry's vote and Father Crepit's usual abstention. It was a wash between Crepit and the council who kindled more disdain in their sulphurous nemesis: Crepit for never taking a stand; the others for standing against everything Lawrence proposed. Like an angry Mt. Saint Helen's, indiscriminately belching toxic particulates, Porphyry spewed recriminations upon his timid confreres, who seemed to be bobbing up and down like lake loons. Trapped, these poltroons did everything but dive for cover to avoid this colleague's invective. Most retreated as far back in their chairs as possible without snapping the hasps.

"I suppose I could expect this from a congeries of academic invalids who have conceded to students everything but a key to the front door! Well, I at least have enough integrity not to countenance any longer this circus called higher education. I intend to resign shortly to avoid staining myself as some stalwarts have done."

What was intended to be a dramatic exit was aborted by Dr. Anita Duessa, respected academician from the nursing department. "I would be the last to keep you in such compromising company, Dr. Porphyry; in fact, I would never forgive myself were I to derail you for a single minute from resigning. However, what I have to say were best spoken now, while your ringing affirmation of this council remains fresh." Dr. Duessa paused briefly, not out of timidity, for she was one of few faculty who remained self-assured under bombardment.

Porphyry gave her a baffled glance. This was not the first time he collided with Anita Duessa whose unflappable nature threw him off balance. More than once in her absence he had alluded to "that strega," or witch, a designation Duessa relished, for she grasped the allusion to her sorceress ancestor. Anita Duessa was petite in stature but a giant in confrontation. While not "pretty," she could boast of several attractive features with the exception of her left eyelid. This drooped like a half closed car hood, leaving her with the wilted gaze of a Parkinson victim. This neural tick was traceable to a dentist's accident five years earlier. Her appointment was routine -- to replace an old filling, but, as the doctor perfunctorily set about injecting her upper jaw with Novocain, and stooping to target the precise place, his back suddenly convulsed. The spasm drove the syringe into the sinus canal. With her trigeminal area under attack, Anita could only moan once before fainting. When she regained consciousness, the stunned dentist, in pain

himself, sputtered an apology, which provided no solace for his anguished patient. Anita's eye remained bruised and tender for several weeks; numbness settled over the entire left side of her face. The effect was a "half mast" eyelid which doctors regretted would never right itself.

Though it was not within the character of Anita Duessa to bring litigation against a long time family dentist, the poor man readily understood when her patronage quietly shifted to a younger, more athletic replacement.

Though not without passion, Anita never permitted sex to upstage her priorities. It was her wolfish independence which Lawrence covertly admired; within the environs of his soul, he nourished an infatuation for her. When Duessa spoke, she was incisive if not clinical. Once, she was challenged by a skeptical student, who preened himself on his ruttish vigor, to "prove that 'survival' is a more potent instinct than sexuality."

"The evidence is obvious; just light a fire in a bed!" she laconically retorted, leaving the irresistible lover to wonder if his question was addressed.

The truth was Anita exercised a vexatious spell over Porphyry, a kind of witchcraft that made him, in his own estimate, disgustingly vulnerable. Duessa, intuiting her magnetism, relished the advantage, and devised a plan to exploit her leverage. With the academic council savoring her comments, she concluded her intervention by adding: "Were you to believe that our vote was as much personal as professional, you would certainly be reading it accurately. Over time, I, for one,

have wearied of your 'scorched earth' tactics which do small credit to you or to this body. In brief, there is no subject you can introduce which isn't tied to your pique, your recklessness. I hope any move you make from Saint Blase's will prove as great a bonus to you as it undeniably will to us." Only when the "strega" had finished did Lawrence careen towards the door, smoldering: "Junkies! Junkies!"

After this imbroglio, which Fr. Crepit delicately referred to a "dialogue we'd well put behind us," Lawrence left the campus hoping to reach home in time to watch the early evening news; there he might take comfort that, whatever television's bleak content, it would pale in comparison to his "hell on earth" at Blase's. It was then, suddenly, memory jarred him that this was the anniversary of his mother's death. The dear woman, the soul of patience, tested, God knows, by her incendiary son, had been released from her travail three years earlier. Out of habit and a peculiar prompting to do the "right thing for mama," Lawrence detoured to scurry into St. Lawrence's parish church. There he went through the "mummery of lighting a candle on her behalf." The cavernous nave was muted in darkness save for vigil lights flanking the high altar whose fiery tongues seemed to fidget and fuss while gossiping about this stranger approaching their shimmering circle. Ignoring the offertory slot, Lawrence saw that all the lamps closest to his patron's statue had been taken. Looking around furtively, he snatched one of the lit candles, exiling it to a "back seat," and in its place substituted his "gift."

He concluded, "On the outside chance this isn't all hokum, I'll be damned if I permit some 'nobody' to mulct me out of 'real estate.'"

Stepping back to admire his tribute, he stood still for one awkward moment, then drifted from the church. Had he stayed, he would have been alarmed to discover that his votive candle's flame, writhing for oxygen, had been snuffed out.

Reaching home, and stowing his briefcase next to the desk, Lawrence noticed that his phone had intercepted a message. The red signal seemed to be blinking more insistently than usual.

"There's nothing so urgent that it can't wait for the news," he grumbled.

But something about the jittery button shouted "Urgent," and he realized that until he satisfied his curiosity he would enjoy no peace, so he snatched the receiver, to learn "what foolishness" could be summoning him away from the tube.

"No doubt some lout wanting tomorrow's assignment, having blithely missed the class when it was announced." Struggling to his feet he sighed: "Well, there will be no peace till I tell him to go to hell on roller skates."

But what was presumed to sate his interest, only teased it more when he learned that Anita Duessa had phoned and would welcome his prompt reply.

Warily dialing Dr. Duessa's number, Lawrence stiffened somewhat when he heard her sepulchral tone. "Yes, this is Lawrence Porphyry, returning your call. Your message sounded urgent, or I wouldn't have replied at this inopportune time."

Anita, betraying no hint of animosity, placidly registered the slight. "Lawrence, I did not wish the evening to slip by without apologizing for my conduct at this afternoon's meeting. With your resignation imminent, I would feel ever so guilty were we to part on inimical terms. I hope you won't think me forward if I ask you on a professional, if not personal, basis to smother any embers of hostility between us. I would be ever so pleased were you to accept an invitation to dinner tomorrow evening. I thought the Sabbath would find us both freed up."

Lawrence's jaw was rotating, but his words only tiptoed around his mouth, giving the impression he was gargling. Finally, he murmured, "Well . . . ah . . . thank you, but I'm not so sure tomorrow isn't taken up . . . My schedule is running at a torrid pace these days."

Duessa, undeterred, pushed ahead, "Oh, I quite understand, and I am ready to adjust my dates to a more convenient time. It's just that I know how weeks can steal by with some of our best resolutions left on 'simmer.' I understand you have a fondness for Chinese cuisine. Following my trip to mainland China last summer, I have perfected, quite satisfactorily, if I do say so, a variety of recipes: Hunan, Szechwan, Mandarin, and Cantonese. I know you would be snared by my Szechwan chicken; it's frightfully hot and spicy, but a wonderful test to any cultivated pallet. And, of course, a glass or two of chilled chablis to douse the fire is a must!"

Porphyry needed no more prompting to acquiesce. His latent attraction to this woman, his

ego's need to be stroked by what was tantamount to a culinary "apology," and his fondness for oriental cookery, all tugged him to surrender. He replied, "Well, with a bit of rearranging I'm sure that I can open my calendar to take you up on a dinner tomorrow. Just set the time and I'll be there."

Anita Duessa never doubted that her invitation would be accepted. Her scenario was unfolding with a saboteur's cunning. All that remained was the purchase of necessary ingredients at the International Market and the best chablis that Antinori vintners could stock on the shelves.

Presiding over a court of condiments, Anita set about transforming, as if by sorcery, some rather simple ingredients into an epicure's rapture: char sui pork roast, massaged in a zesty plumb sauce; abalone, adrift in egg flower soup; large scampi capped with snow peas; and, of course, her promised specialty, chicken Szechwan, zesty and piquant, unique to China's colder provinces.

"I hope Lawrence's taste buds can compete with the sauce's hot peppers, ginger root, and elephant garlic. These feisty fellows can teach anyone how to survive in an oven."

Gazing somewhat wistfully into the waltzing glow of the table candles, Lawrence Porphyry sensed a rare tranquility, almost sedating him.

"I don't know when, if ever, I have experienced a finer meal, a perfect balance of flavors, texture, and company, including this marvelous wine."

As he rhapsodized, he reached for a third portion of Szechwan chicken and also proceeded to empty another fiasco of Antinori chablis.

Anita, the soul of etiquette, added, "Yes, too often we take for granted the alchemy of food and drink to bring people together. Most problems surrender to the knife and fork."

As time glided by, Lawrence grew more voluble, even expansive. His fortifications left unmanned, he commenced to open himself to his resourceful hostess. A litany of suppressed grievances surfaced: Porphyry, the youngster, always ridiculed by peers, a "perennial outsider"; Porphyry, the young man, a stranger to his father.

"I was told, Anita, that his hostility was clear from the beginning. The facts are he didn't even bother to drive my mother and me home from the hospital; instead, my uncle did." As an afterthought, he added, "So, when he left my mother, abandoning me, I felt no grief, as I had no real model to grieve about, only a phantom. Strangely, I never detected a hint of resentment in my mother; in fact, I noted a trace of sympathy which I never could get a handle on."

Anita Duessa stiffened; she arched back as a tennis player about to deliver a stunning serve. "Did it never occur to you that perhaps this man wasn't your real father? That his distance from you was occasioned by the realization that another's affection for your mother had supplanted his own and you were the sign of that detour?"

A shudder seized Lawrence Porphyry as if a grenade had just been tossed onto his plate. In a fraction of a second clouds that had hovered over

his unconscious self drifted apart, revealing a blistering sun which shot ruthless rays upon the guest's head, beams whose clarity only intensified their aggression.

Struggling to gain some semblance of composure, Lawrence snapped, "No . . . No . . . No! That's wild, reckless speculation. Pure rubbish! Blind conjecture."

"No, Lawrence? Blind you say? One of my eyes may look flawed, but its vision is acute. Few are aware that prior to entering the halls of academe at St. Blase's I held a responsible nursing position at Saint Lucy's Hospital, specializing in obstetrics. I well recall a young woman who gave birth, a difficult one at that, to a red haired, pesky son. True it is that your alleged father wasn't there, but her True Love was. You were a termagant even then, crankily declaring your resistance to a meddlesome world. Those few aware of your mother's secret admired the creative name she gave you, 'Lawrence,' which seemed to bond itself to your provocative character. But it's odd that you never probed the mystery of your middle name, 'Ignatius.' Have you never reflected on Ignatius Loyola, the founder of the Jesuit order? That name suggests one 'afire,' and was given you by your real father, a Jesuit, who, loving you at a distance over all these years, has provided a buffer between you and the world. He was responsible for bringing you to Saint Blase's, overseeing your tenure and promotions, and making every effort to put the best face on your outbursts which have earned you much ridicule. And for all this he gained nothing but your contempt. You

interpreted his solicitous moves as weak and craven behavior. Yes, Jason Crepit is your greatest benefactor, your guardian, and, your father."

Lawrence Porphyry found himself standing, feather-headed. His legs felt sodden, like two loaves of doughy bread. His eyes strained in their sockets, rotating freakishly and fixing on no particular object.

"Then . . . then I'm nothing more than a bastard! What a laugh! That's what people have called me as far back as I can remember: Bastard . . . bastard . . . Never dreaming how true their slur really was! Am I now to respond to my so-called 'father'? What 'thanks' to one responsible for the creation of a misfit, a 'scar', mere human wreckage? Should I thank him who has made my self-sufficiency a sick mockery? A joke?"

Anita Duessa, offended to hear this thankless diatribe, prepared to topple this pillar of righteousness; however, before she could mount an attack, Lawrence Ignatius Porphyry bolted from her apartment without so much as slamming the door behind him. Hurling himself into his car, he viciously ripped the pocket of his coat while struggling to tear the keys from it. Reaching home, seething with anger, he threw himself across his bed and gave vent to a firestorm of recrimination.

"I feel dirty . . . sullied with the muck of my mother's life and Crepit's betrayal." In frustration, Lawrence staggered to the shower, intent to scrub himself clean of the mire he felt clinging to him.

Not realizing the irony of what he was saying, he
blurted.

"So much for vows to God . . . fidelity to Him."
The last word caught in his throat. It was to be
Lawrence Ignatius Porphyry's final utterance. A
searing spike pierced his forehead; he wheeled,
twisted, felt himself being sucked into a tunnel.
As he tumbled, his arm slammed into the dial
regulating water temperature. A scalding, steady
spray pelted his body, a blistering second baptism!

Anita Duessa found his scorched, swollen
corpse the following day, having phoned repeatedly
earlier. The body looked as if it had been basted
and roasted in a microwave, but the face,
peculiarly, seemed unscathed; almost an irenic
look masked it, a gaze emancipated from struggle,
an expression at once fresh and reconciled.

To this day, the professor of nursing, before the
shrine of St. Lawrence, periodically lights a candle,
murmuring a small prayer on behalf of that
patron's stilled son. The flame, it seems to her,
nimbly scampers about the taper, tormenting the
wick, and glowing with a candescence all its own.

Saint Calixtus' Ear
Digging the Last Grave

𝓛ittle escaped the hawk-like notice of Tad Rully, now in his twelfth year as resident gravedigger at Saint Calixtus' Cemetery -- that barrow for the diocese of Superior, Wisconsin, which includes such promising towns as Cornucopia and Cloverland, just a rock skip from the Canadian border. Local "diggers" of another sort pronounce gravely that this enclave of shovels and mounds derives its name from the venerable catacomb on Rome's Via Appia. Its bowels had welcomed hundreds of Nero's martyred Christians -- hushed ancestors of Calixtus' present residents.

Tad was christened "Theodore" at the insistence of a pious mother. Like Sarah, she had borne barrenness until, as she saw it, "God gave" this son whose precious arrival into the world was to be oddly committed to others' departure from it. To say that Tad excelled in his vocation is not overstatement. The record reveals one who, other than suffering through two weeks of yearly vacation, had missed only five work days in his long tenure. "He's a sturdy one," chuckled his Uncle Emery. "That's from working close to the soil!" And with a well-creased snicker he chortled, "I don't think he'll ever give up the ghost!"

Tad, like an Exocet, targeted a white stationery note which aimlessly fluttered from the purse of a woman grieving, who, supported on the plump arm of Monsignor Willard J. Pouter, stumbled from the

canopied gravesite towards her limousine. The Lincoln was parked three hundred feet away, dominating like a Doberman an elbow of road bordered by three sullen yew trees. The caretaker scurried to the delicate paper, noticed the prestigious law firm's name on it, then smoothly managed to thrust a personal note into the teary woman's hand. She continued to dab at her eyes, but in her agitation began using the exchanged token instead of the missive which accidentally escaped from her bag. The confusion portended an irony only time would ripen.

Monsignor Pouter, the solicitous escort who observed this muddle, was a porcine prelate, a native of Wisconsin, whose fervent devotion to its cheese had shaped him, finally, into a sphere not unlike a cheddar wheel. His loping gait had earned him the sobriquet "Barge" from his clerical associates. He repaid their attention by cultivating a rigid smile that one might read on the slit lips of a gout victim standing in an interminable smorgasbord line. But that frozen crease was not his only artifice; he also managed to shepherd a flock whose precarious state of soul was relieved somewhat by the stable state of their securities. Among these needy and needed clients Ms. Astoria Flushing, the aggrieved lady, could certainly be numbered.

Born Elsie Madsen, sole daughter of a logger and companion who survived on the rugged north coast of Washington State, Astoria resolved young to leave the Evergreen State for lusher pastures. This she successfully accomplished after her senior year of high school, with the assistance of a floater,

a stubby marmot-like youth, five years older than his new ally. His affluent father provided him the liberty to roam through life with few obligations save addressing the needs of Nature and occasionally intercepting a healthy subsidy to perpetuate his pilgrimage. Lester Ellison clumsily cultivated the aura of a political apostate, eons ahead of his time, who, "in principle," stood aloof from his country's demands. "I'm not dying for nobody!" he would solemnly announce, convinced that his every utterance enjoyed a Delphic eminence, competitive with anything in Greek tragedy.

To be sure, Elsie ignored Lester's sour "patriotism," but supported religiously his creed of comfort through others. This tenet she, too, devoutly embraced, pledging never to renounce it.

Lester and Elsie's relationship did not pulsate with passion; any titillation focused on travel. For five years the two confederates strolled along the trestle of distraction, on a junket which provided resourceful Elsie with an advanced "degree" in aping the gentility and studied insouciance of the rich. "Classrooms" varied from the languid elegance of Hawaii's "Pink Palace," whose tanned and pampered denizens made lethargy respectable, to Rome's fashionable Via Condotti, where profusions of raw silk cascaded from every window, complemented by supple mounds of lambskin gloves and soft, brocaded purses. These lured the logger's daughter to bond completely with affluent refinement.

But Lester's obscene death brought all "theatre" to a brutal halt! Majorca's Costa del Calma

ironically hosted the savagery: a victim trussed up like Saint Sebastian, patron of pin-makers. The young man's punctured carcass testified to an exit as hard as its journey had been easy. To Palma's chief inspector it would appear that the killer had methodically perforated the lad's body with a blade like a letter opener's, until the victim's teased flesh succumbed to shock and gory ventilation. It was also Christmastide and the plaza fronting the Cathedral had recently seen squadrons of merry youngsters break open the traditional piñata, spilling its contents of sweetmeats into eager hands -- youths soon to be aware of a crime whose malign nature would provide a grotesque comparison with their innocent frolic.

At the time of this outrage Elsie, solo, was touring Toledo, thrilling to El Greco's genius, including his "Martyrdom of Saint Sebastian," as well as to that Mecca's wondrously filigreed swords, daggers, and letter-openers. Her incredulity, indeed, near shock, were unmistakable when the repulsive news jolted her serenity. She rushed to Barcelona; once there, with remarkable composure, she made final departure arrangements -- the last of her travels with Lester. His porous remains she would take back to his father, whose periodic subsidy, if already mailed, would have to be designated "Return to Sender," since "Please Forward," would be quite out of the question.

Monsignor Pouter presumably was the only confidant who knew of Astoria's name change. With some compunction she disclosed to him her "flirtation with vanity" while in Europe some years

earlier. This revelation was quietly divulged at a
soirée -- one of several hosted by the cleric, who
stoutly affirmed that "parties and penitents were
as complementary as scotch and soda." With ease,
the good father would stir waves of remorse on the
normally placid seas of his prodigals' souls. One
such ripple ruffled Astoria, who mused that her
life may have been tinctured with pride -- a flaw
she felt, which her recording angel could not
ignore.

A side benefit accrued to Pouter's unique
apostolate. By overseeing extirpation of guilt in
others, he was spared from dwelling on any need
to rescue himself. In a word, God's servant had
invested in a rewarding brand of "liberation
theology" which larded him with consolation by
doting on others' aberrations; this tactic obviated
uneasy confrontation with closer, personal
mischief.

"Astoria," Elsie allowed, was chosen for a most
pragmatic reason: it recalled a town in her native
Northwest which she easily associated with
prestige and furs. Her surname was another
matter; its origin had nothing to do with New
York's lucrative "Meadows," but owed its selection
to her father's proclivity for poker. She realized
any gambler considered a "flush" an unqualified
stroke of success, which one would do well to
weave into a family fabric and thereby win favor of
any who admire status.

A leaden setting it was when Astoria Flushing
stepped from Concourse F and introduced herself
to Lester's father, whose devastation at his son's
loss seemed oddly inconsistent with the prolonged

and mutual separation the two enjoyed for almost a decade. Brushing aside this puzzle, Astoria appeared the epitome of solicitude. The senior Ellison, a widower, was struck by her sweetness and poise -- sensations of softness, he had imagined, long buried with his wife.

The memorial Mass, a simple liturgy for a wandering son of the church, was celebrated by the redoubtable Monsignor Pouter. When he finally intoned: "May the angels lead you into Paradise. May the martyrs greet you at your coming," Astoria, never tardy to seize an advantage and pestered with the prospect of any deprivation, determined to approach the priest for directions to those celestial shores which seemed more than competitive with anything she had luxuriated in on a mundane level. Incorporation into the "fullness of faith" happened later when cleansing baptismal water trickled across her forehead, moistening a pearl necklace which sparkled joyously for the occasion.

Burton Ellison, dredging up a courtliness which had slumbered following his wife's "sleep" and his second "marriage" to Business, was not slow to insist that Astoria remain as his house guest, following his boy's interment, where always diligent Tad, the gravedigger, uncharacteristically lingered over his task. Astoria readily accepted her host's invitation, and thus, began a relationship which resembled in many ways Tristan and Isolt's. Each couple relished not a marriage, but a mirage, muted love at best which flourished more in separation than union. It all ended, as the troubadours promised, in that

inevitable and choicest separation, where fondness really blossoms, namely, in death.

Astoria, like a dutiful and committed wife, ever protective and efficient, heaped on her idol undivided attention; he, in turn, experienced a happiness long presumed vagrant. She coaxed and mobilized his hopes, which, if not realistic, were flattering. Even in business matters, the formerly imperious executive, who ruled his company like a desert emir, increasingly deferred to his "darling's advice and schemes." All this gave his business associates pause. Eyebrows, like a Nikon shutter, blinked in stupefaction at the "Boss's treasure," who, in four years, prospered in every sense, including that of major beneficiary.

"Time," seemed to mellow and grant a generous reprieve to Ellison. His renewed vigor escaped no one, including the "Gem of his life," always doting at his side. What a shock then to read in the Monday morning Monitor: "Wealthy Executive Crushed in Bizarre Mishap." Though it took time to sort through the tangle of details, a terrifying picture emerged.

Astoria and Burton were relaxing for a weekend at their secluded country lodge, which, for weeks now, had been groaning and fidgeting under extensive remodeling -- all, of course, scrutinized by the "Lady of the house." Apparently, Ellison had retired to his den with its extensive library. Detectives guessed that, as he reached for a volume of Gibbon's *Decline and Fall of the Roman Empire,* an entire section of shelving broke free of its hasp, tumbling thunderously upon him. The considerable weight crushed him like a wafer.

"One sprawling contusion," the coroner blurted to police.

When chaos had subsided and the heap was cleared, the victim was found still clutching the final volume of Gibbon, as if some tidy imp orchestrated the fall of both "empires," before each slipped away.

Astoria, who was upstairs at the time, rushed to the clamor; peering in, she found herself numb beyond belief, paralyzed even to call Emergency immediately. No matter. Death was instant. The culprit hasp, it was deduced, must have jarred loose in protest of all the hammering and sawing which had rocked the residence in recent weeks.

Thus it happened that Burton Ellison's "young wife" now became "The Lady," undisputed heiress of his fortune. The widow's grief was assuaged by prosperity; remorse yielded to revenue. However, the prize would not remain uncontested for long: "No man is an island," and an Island would verify how contingent "success" is; how downright unstable struts one's future.

Majorca, some scholars insist, nurtured the soul of Spain's original inhabitants. These are the proud Catalan people, who stubbornly cling to their language and culture against all efforts to plant them into Spanish soil. Dispossessed of wealth and power, many manage to hold fast to a noble heritage, eager to vindicate honor when trivialized, or worse, exposed to ridicule. Into this category fits Ruiz Sanson Narvaez. He it was, as matters curdled, who penned a revealing letter in fractured English to a stranger, "Mr. Tad Rully." This note was posted shortly before a spider tumor

mortally entangled Narvaez's faculties and dispatched him to Judgment. Ruiz wrote this message not to effect some kind of reconciliation with his Maker; rather, it served as a kind of "radiation" to combat another "cancer," more virulent, one which invaded his heart and had been gnawing at its tissue for some time. With one like Ruiz Narvaez in mind, *Ecclesiasticus* cautions: "Laugh no man to scorn in the bitterness of his soul."

As tourists know, Majorca boasts of its "Hermitage," symbol of passion, where George Sand and Chopin consumed each other in requited love. A pity their fervor left frigid a solitary Elsie Madsen, who, earlier, as an ingenuous pilgrim, was visiting this paradise, intending to rendezvous with Lester and his "check book" shortly thereafter. In her own "grotto" she met and was courted by Ruiz and seemed to repay his fervor with every favor short of a promise to marry.

"Impossible!" she shuddered, coyly suggesting she was another's chattel, brutally intimidated by a degenerate, older escort, who terrorized her, had stalked her like a plague, infecting her desire to live, let alone love. The outraged, impulsive Catalan, as eager to revenge his "Lady Love" as to rescue her, concluded, incorrectly, that final severance from her "tormentor" would emancipate the prize for him. Thus a permanent exit, at the hands of Ruiz Sanson Narvaez, awaited Lester Ellison, who must have expired with as much puzzlement as pain.

However, the murdered victim's mortal wound was not isolated; the Majocam "liberator" too was

"sacrificed," when Elsie, after her "savior's" heroics, coolly discarded him. The crime done, an obstacle removed, and a golden opportunity beckoning her, Astoria Flushing skipped from Lester's itinerant world of subsidies to substance; namely, to security found in a vulnerable and pliant widower, who had just lost a son. Astoria's stratagem was bold and manipulating, but, like Washington State's rugged coastline, not without reefs and an angry surf to threaten smooth passage.

Emulous of the Old World's affection for its rich past, the New World, more modestly, hugs its briefer history. Records, even school yearbooks, abound, extensively providing a credible tether to time. If one were to peruse such a record preserved on the bookshelf of Tad Rully for over twenty years, a provocative truth would emerge, scrawled across the face of a young man's grinning picture: "All the best! To my only friend! Lots of 'Lady Luck' Forever! Les Ellison." Yes Lester, the truant rich man's son, and Tad, gift to a barren mother, were, for any who could remember, inseparable, even when distance played the spoiler. Occasional correspondence, familiar and warm, such as the one which the outsider, hapless Ruiz Narvaez, ripped from his dying victim's shirt, clearly testified to an unique bond. Over time, with Elsie's taunting repudiation always before him, Ruiz, the spurned "hero," and stranger to them all, curiously culled, scanned, even memorized Tad's letter to Lester; in fact, the now cancer-wasted Majorcan felt as close to Tad Rully, as, in fact, was the letter's murdered recipient. A

freakish sympathy surfaced in Ruiz born of a scalding revenge, which urged an alliance with the gravedigger, ratified by a "gift" of rich information. It was this perversely pure token, exposing the real Astoria and her treacherous ambition, which Tad squeezed into a "grieving" widow's hand at the gravesite, embellished only by a phone number and signed: "Theodore Rully."

To this day, bewildered townsfolk chatter in disbelief at the unlikely marriage between the sexton and the heiress. Memory of the wedding Mass remains as fresh as were the autumn mums which winked smartly from the main altar of Poor Souls' Church. Monsignor Pouter, dipping into deep reservoirs of accommodation which must have taxed even his limber conscience, gazed on the curious couple. With an inquiring eye, roving particularly over Theodore, he quoted Christ's words from Saint John:

I shall not call you servants anymore, because a servant does not know his master's business; I call you friends, because I have made known to you everything I learned from my Father.

This assurance, from the apostle "whom Jesus loved," seemed to illumine the groom's face into something seraphic. Finally, the portly celebrant favored a glance at the bride, who knelt composed before him. Moved by her solemnity, he invoked the final blessing:

May you find happiness and satisfaction in your work. May daily problems never cause you undue

anxiety, nor the desire for earthly possessions dominate your life. But may your heart's first desire be always of the good things waiting for you in the life of heaven.

Astoria, usually resilient, betrayed no radiant emotion during or following the liturgy, only what was a placidity interpreted as reserved joy. "Not improper," some reflected, "for one whose short life had known such grief." Elsie, an opportunist who always preferred an accommodating vice to an obstinate virtue, considered it tolerable to alter her name from "Flushing" to "Rully."

"Astoria Rully," she sighed. "Perhaps . . . 'Flushing' was too much like a game of risk. Rully . . . Rully . . . Astoria Rully!' It does have a chime to it not altogether inelegant."

Tad, for his part, grew quietly genial, with the unassuming smile of an Assisi among his swallows. Retired, obviously at peace with God and His world, he was regularly seen ensconced behind the wheel of his new Lincoln as it meandered lazily into the country setting of his former labors, Saint Calixtus' Cemetery. There, routinely, he would pause before one particular plot, nod, smile, and move on to the marbled presence of Saint Calixtus himself. For his ears alone, he would whisper a prayer of thanksgiving, grateful to have dug his last grave . . . .

About the Author

James G. Powers, S.J., is a Jesuit priest. He is a professor of English at Gonzaga University, a senior member of the English Department and its former chairman. He also holds a position on the University Board of Members and the Coughlin Chair of English Studies. His specialties are 17th and 18th Century British Literature and Philology. Publications include: *A Cultivated Vocabulary* and *Handbook of Helpers*; fiction in *The Washington Anthology* (1989 Centennial Edition) and *Amelia*; articles in *Studies in Short Fiction, Human Development,* and *The Bible Today.* His favorite prose authors are Henry Fielding, Walker Percy, Flannery O'Connor and P.D. James.